THE AMAZING TALES

OF

MIKE O'DONOVAN

1st Edition, 2003
2nd Edition, 2005
This Edition, 2006

Also By the same author:

Short Tall Tales
Timmy & The Dragon
Cormac, King of the Leprechauns

Published by:
Blarney Publications
44 Haldene Avenue
Bishopstown
Cork
Tel: 00 353 21 4530422
        00 353 86 2849843

Editing: Jack O'Malley

Printed by: City Print - 021-4545655

ISBN: 0-9543530-0-5

Contents

Preface

Except where otherwise, all words in this book are in plain simple language. There are a number of words at times contained in different stories, such as 'Cafe' and 'Leprechaun' which are not entirely kosher - for this we apologise.

All characters depicted in this book are totally fictitious. Any references to similar persons living, dead, or otherwise are purely coincidental, except in some stories where I wanted to exact revenge on some people who I know to be ruthless, lying bastards, but they are only a small minority. Otherwise, everything in the garden is rosy and all of the stories are of a gentle non-offensive nature, except for some of the more grisly sickening yarns, which some of you might find a little bit on the gory and ghoulish side. Wimps!

Mike O'Donovan

For my sister, Betty,
with all my love.

Laughing Matters

M17

One of the long legs of Janet Sutton-Hallmark lay atop the mahogany desk. With nail clippers in hand she deftly trimmed the purple coloured nails of her toes. Gilbert Spoon stood opposite her with a large ashtray in hand ready to catch the flying toenails as they whizzed through the air, the nervous tic in his left eye accelerating to maximum speed in his excitement.

Janet was the head of the British Secret Service, having slept in many beds in many positions to attain her present position. Gilbert was her adoring second in command and secretly loved Janet, but Janet looked down on Gilbert, she being six foot, five inches tall and her admirer was just over five feet.

There was a secret knock on the secret door and Jeremy Silkcutt-Blink (known as Smoky to all) entered, followed by his sidekick Sam Snyde. Sam Snyde was a joy - not to behold. His long acned face seemed never to end, stretching back over his bald shining head, finishing some place above the back of his neck. Jeremy's monocle dropped from his right eye on seeing so much of his superior's long leg exposed on the desk, covering a document marked 'Top Secret.'

Jeremy's nostrils quivered with disgust, he not having a liking for women, and also resenting her position as head of all of the spooks, a job he felt he was far more qualified to do. Jeremy had also slept with many of the hierarchy in his attempts at promotion, but shit was his thanks.

Gilbert Spoon was busily engaged trying to open a bottle of nail varnish as Janet Sutton-Hallmark daintily flicked the 'Top Secret' document across the desk with her foot and addressed Jeremy's contorted face. *"Read,"* she said, indicating to Spoon and taking the nail varnish from him. With one twist she easily loosened the bottle top and with the same nail-clipped foot indicated the door to her visitors.

Taking the document from her desk, Sam Snide swiftly passed it into the hands of his boss, Silkcutt Blink. Clicking their heels in unison, they turned and marched out through the door. Luckily, it was still open!

Jeremy's minion, Sam, read it out to him. It was the dossier on one Cedric Morehamption, Commander and Social Events organiser of the Irish Republican Army.

The Hon. Cedric Morehampton was born in Southampton, so to avoid confusion and to satisfy his longing to be more Irish than the Irish themselves, he changed his name to Seamus De Valera-Collins, took up step-dancing (winning many medals), baked sodabread, played the pipes (badly), and tried hard to speak with an Irish accent but failed miserably to cover up his clipped English accent.

One night while singing Republican songs of a bloody nature, in a pub, he was approached by two drunken men and offered the post of I.R.A. leadership, they explaining that the previous leader had given his life for Ireland by falling into a waterlogged sandpit at his local golf club, drowning to death. Cedric Morehamption accepted with alacrity and pride. Ergo, an English aristocrat and ex-member of Alcoholics Anonymous became Supreme Commander of the I.R.A.

The Irish police failed completely to uncover the murky goings on of the same Commander. His first brilliant scheme was to introduce shift work at a local bomb-making factory emulating another great Irishman Henry Ford, who actually introduced factory shiftwork to the world, in his marvellous wisdom. Striking, poorly paid workers were shot to death on Henry's orders and the wheels of industry kept turning. Henry Ford was a great Irishman.

The two twelve-hour shifts operated from the back room of a local crèche and the comings and goings of groups of men and women entering and leaving at eight in the morning and twenty hundred hours in the evening, cunningly disguised in balaclava helmets, ensured that nobody ever suspected a thing.

The problem was totally unforeseen - overproduction! The hidden bunkers were now full to overflowing and Cedric's soldiers were also complaining about the erratic working hours and lack of sleep. There were talks of a strike and mounting a picket outside the crèche. The I.R.A. was a non-union organisation and it was felt that the fucker with the English accent was abusing that fact.

Everything about Cedric was included in the dossier. Photographs of him from his tall-hatted youth at Eton to his days as a long-haired, pot-smoking, bandana-wearing hippy with his arms around a turbaned gentleman of obvious Indian extraction who bore a look of knowledge and understanding on his smiling and podgy face.

The establishment did not suffer traitors gladly. Cedric was to land in deep shit.

The reports from agents in the Irish Republic indicated that the traitor with the codename 'Mudas' (the arm on the typewriter bearing the letter J did not work), was a dangerous man and would have to be watched.

The two English spies collecting the waste bins were a source of much interest among the local people. The explanation that they were taking part in a European Exchange Scheme was accepted in good faith. People were surprised and not a little envious to be informed by the two Englishmen, that the usual men were now on bin-collecting duties on the Riveria, it all being part of the effort towards European Integration.

The bin-find was at first disappointing - a tomato-ketchup-soiled paper on set dancing, explaining all of the movements and steps. An end-piece of soft-boiled bacon with strips of smelly cabbage attached. A little piece of tail-end of corned beef and a little crushed floury potato. All of this proved that Cedric Morehampton had certainly gone native, but the last salvaged item clinched the whole thing. It was a book detailing English misdeeds in Ireland going back hundreds of years and the two spies read this book of obvious fiction with incredulity. The book was written by a prominent English historian.

They rang London on their secret mobile phone using their secret code and informed their superiors of the important find and also suggesting that a tail be put on the author of the said book, one Gweneth Teebone-Lake. Obviously Gweneth was another Mudas.

The British Prime Minister faced Janet Sutton-Hallmark across his large desk, pausing only to press the concealed button controlling the miniature railway system which ran around the desk top. They both waited and watched until the last cargo train stopped at a siding marked 'Goods' before getting down to the nitty gritty of solving the nation's secret problems.

Ernie Lipton found Janet's Sloan Square accent quite irritating. More than that, he was well aware of how she had bedded her way to her position as head of M17, the Secret Secret Service. While he had had to knock at many doors talking to all sorts of people promising them the moon just to get elected, then the infighting to achieve leadership. Across from him was the very tall figure of Sutton-Hallmark who had used the bed to make nearly double his salary.

Premier Lipton joined his hands together and put on his most serious look (well practised in front of his mirror every morning), and politely asked Janet to stop chewing the gum, which she did, sticking it under the desk.

Janet's written report was short and very much to the point. "Too many Blacks." "Too many Chinese." "Too many colours which were not white." "Too many scroungers and layabouts." Premier Lipton noted that there was no mention of the Irish or of Ireland.

"What about the Irish question?" Lipton asked Janet. Janet sighed a sigh of exasperation and annoyance, the heat of the room at No. 10 Downing Street was causing one of her false eyelashes to droop. Attempting to maintain composure she blinked, causing a little more

of the lash to hang down, nearly covering her right eye. *"That,"* she said haughtily, *"is top secret."*

Prime Minister Lipton's face was reddening and expanding with temper (showing some quite interesting veins protruding from his fat neck). *"I am the fucking Prime Minister, I can see everything."* Janet was fast! *"I beg to differ, SIR. Even with the best eyesight in the world nobody can see everything."* Only when Ernie threatened to have her arrested did she deign to part with a report marked 'Top Top Secret,' and appropriately titled 'The Irish Question.'

Janet was into her third strip of bubble gum by the time Ernie finished reading the report. The right eyelash was barely hanging in there and the left lash was now adopting the same journey as the one on the right, but if there had been bets on, the right would have won hands down.

"This is serious shit," exclaimed the leader of Britain and Northern Ireland. *"We have a guerilla in our mist."* He knew well that Cedric Collins De Valera or whatever he called himself was not really in their mist, but thought that exclamation sounded very Prime Ministerial. He decided to say it again only this time he would say it with raised eyebrows whilst holding his chin at the same time. *"Yes this is serious shit indeed."*

Looking at Janet he could see that his impression of a serious man had impressed her. The very first meeting with the then new head of M17 had not gone very well. Ernie Lipton had been one of the speakers to be asked to a debate at the Oxford Union, the topic being 'Socialism and the Rights of Man.' As a member of a party with a very slight leaning in the direction of socialism, Ernie led a panel professing an inclination in that area.

Janet Sutton-Hallmark led the opposing team, she masquerading as a member of a hockey team from the Outer Hebrides.

Janet's team won. Even though her short talk on how the rich were nicer people, spoken in an atrocious Scottish accent did not win her many plaudits, the flashing of her knickers did. The resultant vote was a forgone conclusion. Ernie felt very sore about the result, even though he did not care much about socialism, he did not like to lose to somebody from Scotland.

"We have a team in Ireland right now, using alibis." She meant Aliases but Ernie's education had been at the University of Cunning and he nodded his head sagely, none the wiser.

"And? And?" he asked briskly. Janet had recently finished reading a tome titled 'How To Be A Spy,' written by the Director of Operations during the successful Bay of Pigs Invasion and had learned a lot from it, also some very useful buzz words.

"Our operatives on the turf (code name for Ireland) report daily to control and are at an advanced stage in the process of having Mudas sequestered."

Ernie Lipton nodded his head and tried to look grave and comprehending. He was very impressed with that sort of talk. It did not matter about understanding. What the fuck was an operative?

"Excellent work, my dear, carry on." Taking this as a dismissal, Janet walked to the door. On exiting she heard the sound of the train-set starting up again and the Prime Minister going *"Toot, toot."*

Jeremy Silkcutt-Blink sat at the wheel of the refuse truck watching Sam Snyde in the rearview mirror. Only yesterday he had scolded Sam for not replacing the wheelie bins back to the exact position from where they had been collected. Jeremy hated slovenly work and believed in doing a job, any job, properly, whether it was collecting people's waste or killing them. Jeremy was fairly fastidious in his outlook. His acquaintances at work said this sprung from the fact that Jeremy came from a broken home. The first cracks appearing when he was aged ten, the house eventually falling down around his family, they barely escaping with their lives. It was an old house.

Sam Snyde was thoroughly sick of this assignment, despite numerous requests Jeremy would not allow him to drive the truck, claiming seniority and quoting sub-section six, paragraph eleven which in effect, made Sam Snyde, Jeremy's serf. What sickened him more were Jeremy's remarks about Sam looking more the part of a binman.

The complaints from the overflowing bunker owners were easily solved, Cedric copied the Brits and started exporting. Of course the I.R.A. could not match the British in supplying weapons of mass destruction, but as Cedric Seamus pointed out *"from small acorns ..."* etc.

Jeremy sat in the cab reading the social pages of 'The Times' while Sam waded through the collected debris in the back, seeking goodies, when a car stopped and two men got out, calling Sam from the back and addressing them both reading from a letter, *"Seamus Collins De Valera told me to tell you that he wants you back at his house now to partake of tea, you have an hour. If you decide not to avail of this hospitable offer, it will be the last decision you will ever make. Best wishes, S.C. De Valera."*

Two minutes and thirty four seconds later there was a pounding on the front door of the house of Cedric Seamus.

The offer from the I.R.A. was very simple. *"Work for us or we shoot you to fuck."* It was an offer the two English spies could not refuse.

That same day Jeremy Silkcutt-Blink ordered the bald acned one called Sam to send a message to love-struck Gilbert Spoon who read it out to his lovely longlegged superior and the cause of many of his naughty dreams, Janet Sutton-Hallmark, who immediately sent a copy by pigeon post to the very common Prime Minister who immediately called a Cabinet Meeting.

The room at No. 10 Downing Street was soon filled with every member of the Cabinet, all despising their leader nearly as much as he despised them. They all despised each other as well. Despite all of the despising the meeting got off to a friendly start.

Ernie Lipton's face was flush red and expanding, his veins attempting to flaunt themselves again, fascinating the other members of the cabinet.

Ernie's information was skimpy as to the source, lest any of his Cabinet be a Mudas in the mist.

"Our two top agents in Ireland were able to surround a local battalion of the bold I.R.A. and after a prolonged gun battle our boys succeeded in killing three hundred and twenty-two of them before capturing the head of that murderous organisation. Sadly, the head of that same said branch of extremist fanatical kamikaze fuckers is from what we like to call mainland Britain. In point of truth, he is English."

There was stunned silence in the room. No member of the Cabinet had ever heard their Premier use the word 'Fuckers' before, not in the plural anyway. This business about killing hundreds of Irish killers seemed to be too good to be true, knowing the reputation of the spooks. But their boss had spoken and nobody wanted to lose their portfolios. So, as one, they rose from their chairs, the sober ones noticeably faster than the majority, and applauded their leader with clapping and whistling. A passenger carriage toppled over and fell from the desk onto the deep shag carpet.

Jeremy could not fail but to notice that some householders threw out some items in nearly perfect condition. After instructing Sam to sort out the wheat from the chaff, he sold on the more acceptable and not so smelly pots and pans, clothing, in fact anything that would be bought, making him a nice little earner on the side. His favourite stop was at the crèche, in whose bin were to be found the most lucrative and interesting items. Always loads of wiring and metal objects shaped like mortars and other steel bits and pieces. Jeremy considered putting a second truck on the road.

"Tap, tap, tap," it stopped and then restarted, *"tap, tap, tap."* Seamus Collins De Valera thought for a minute before eventually deciding that it must be the front door and concluded that because of the

knocking on that particular door, the chances were that there must be someone outside. His logic proved to be spot on, because on opening the said door he was faced with the majestic and broad figure of the English writer, and winner of the nineteen-seventy beauty contest held at Bovine-On-Sea, Gweneth Teebone-Lake. Holding out her hand Gweneth said quietly *"Cedric Morehamption I presume."* She was quickly ushered in (pushed actually, but ushered sounds better).

Cedric Seamus tried to hide away his knitting needles and the balls of wool but the attempt was futile as they fell back out of the overstuffed oven (he was cooking a turkey at the time).

Producing a single A4 size sheet of paper from her bosom area, Gweneth Teebone-Lake read from it.

"Janet Sutton-Hallmark and her sidekick, Gilbert Spoon of M17 ridded themselves of the opposition by dispatching Jeremy Silkcutt-Blink and his assistant Sam Snyde to Ireland to seek you out and murder you to death."

Cedric Smith asked, with ashen face, *"How, how, how?"* sounding like a delegate at a native American Convention, before trodding on a knitting needle, then getting his legs entwined in the looped strands of wool, causing him to stumble back on top of the hot oven, causing some burning to his rear end. *"How did you find out? And how do you know?"*

Gweneth opened her mouth and smiled, showing rows of gleaming cracked teeth, *"How I know is nobody's business, and even the blind dogs in the street know that the two boys from London are driving around collecting rubbish, and might even open a junk yard or recycling business."*

Cedric was struck dumb by all of this (he wasn't really, it only being a figure of speech). But his ashen face was slowly lighting up again.

"Those English bastards," he wailed. After being reminded by his visitor that he was also English, Cedric started again *"Those bastards."*

Cedric was lucky to have remained as leader since the near strike at the crèche. Long drawn-out negotiations resulted in a victory for the men. Shiftwork was now banned and volunteers worked thirty-eight and a half hours per week with time and a half for Saturdays and double pay for Sundays.

The 'Scorpion' held both hands in front of the fireplace, occasionally rubbing them together, forgetting completely that he had neglected to light a fire, but the brandy he sipped (glugging now and again) made him warm enough. The laughter which poured out of him could be compared only to that of a paid mourner at a wake (but who is perfect?). He laughed that weird laugh again and muttered to himself, *"The fools"* (he had nobody else to talk to). The 'Scorpion' was the puppeteer and all of the rest were mere puppets, Hallmark, Blink, Silkcutt, Snyde, Cedric, the lot. He was pulling the strings and they all danced to his tune.

The 'Scorpion' retired from the room, moving sideways, as was his wont, singing happily to himself. He knew all the words of 'Puppet on A String,' and, in fairness, he had a handy voice. If there had been anybody there to listen to his singing, they would have enjoyed it.

The unexpected death of Seamus Collins De Valera was much regretted by the peasants of the Dark Valley (there are no peasants and no Dark Valley in this story but if I do not use the above this paragraph could be very boring). Thousands of mourners followed behind his coffin (nine people). The eulogy delivered by Fidel Castro (of Castro's Fish and Chip Emporium of Sallynoggin), drew tears to the eyes of many people (there was a biting wind). Carloads of police mounted a military type operation, completely surrounding the cemetery (there were two policemen watching the proceedings from an unmarked car, one of them was asleep).

The Coroner's Report read out at the inquest made for frighteningly sad news for any Irish person. Overdosing on cabbage and Irish step-dancing was a rare occurrence. Some of those attending the inquest consoled themselves that he was English and really had not built up any resistance to the deadly combination of his short time in the Island of Saints and Scholars.

In a biography of Cedric Morehamption, Seamus Collins De Valera, published many years later, it was alleged that Cedric's real reason for leaving England was to avoid Morris Dancing and the associated hats, bells, waving handkerchiefs and jumping men. Interviews with Cedric's childhood neighbours and friends proved this allegation to be correct.

Cedric left a cabbage-stained typewritten note which was found by a man delivering curly greens.

The note pleaded with the ordinary rank and file to accept Cedric's nomination of Jeremy Silkcutt-Blink as Supreme Commander of the Irish Republican Army. The note went on to praise Silkcutt-Blink and his monacle, as a lover of Ireland and all things Irish and noted Jeremy Silkcutt-Blink's solemn promise to learn step-dancing.

The vote to elect Silkcutt-Blink as the new Commander was unanimous except for the votes of some I.R.A. members who were on holidays, taking advantage of cheap flights to the Costa Blanca (fares were down by ten per cent due to cancellations in that area, because of a serious outbreak of cholera. There were great bargains to be had!).

The 'Scorpians' act of murder on Cedric involved stuffing him with soft-boiled cabbage and making him dance at the same time. Stuffing, dancing, stuffing, dancing, the torture went on for hours until Cedric could take no more cabbage, being stuffed to the gills. In his final dance of death he managed one little last tap before sinking to the floor of his newly scrubbed kitchen, cabbage pouring from his mouth.

Cedric's last thoughts and wishes were that he hoped the cabbage involved was not G.M.

The death of Janet Sutton-Hallmark was equally gruesome. Whilst dancing at her usual club on a Saturday night, she chanced very near the band, her mouth open as she sang loudly, knowing all the words of "How Much Is That Doggy In The Window,' when a clarinet was shoved down her throat. Despite every effort the instrument stuck solid. Janet died within half an hour, suffering a very slow and tuneful death. The musical offender was never found.

Gilbert Spoon was promoted to the position of head of M17. He owed the promotion to the illustrious Prime Minister Ernie Lipton who rooted for him, brushing aside the protestations of the Minister for Defence Bertram Toncell, and in a very short time Gilbert Spoon was installed in the (lowered) swivel chair previously occupied by the lovely and late Jane Sutton-Hallmark. He felt his face and bald head, hoping that promotion might help to rid him of the scourge of the left eyed tic.

The 'Scorpion' sat at his desk and contemplated life and death. The simple act of writing that book under the pseudonym 'Gweneth Teebone-Lake' had proven to be an act of inspired brilliance. He now had an easily handled monacled twit as head of the I.R.A. and an undersized manageable nail catcher as head of M17. In other words, he controlled two opposing forces. Depending on the polls, he could have a bomb set off any time, then ride to the rescue and up the popularity of the government, securing them for another term.

He thought about the possibilities of a holiday, maybe even going back to Ireland, only this time he would not have to dress as a woman, or endure the smell of the awful boiled cabbage.

The 'Scorpion' had stood in the dancehall with the crowd circling the writhering dying person of Janet Sutton-Hallmark and felt a twinge of remorse, she, in fact might have achieved success as a clarinet player, judging by her swan-song. Janet had died note perfect.

All the maudlin thought of deaths, and more to come, were starting to depress the 'Scorpion', so he turned his mind to the important business at hand and flicked the switch which turned on the model railway system which covering his ministerial desk. This was real life. *"Toot, toot!"*

Cream Rises

George sat at the enormous desk in the Oval Office for the first time and observed his surroundings through naturally glazed eyes.

George Senior had always told him that he would one day follow in Daddy's footsteps and he accepted this statement as readily as he accepted largesse from people Daddy told him were friends who therafter would have to be compensated for their loyalties.

After requesting one of his aides to open his fly (he resolved to master that difficult task one day), George went to the presidential bathroom and urinated on the floor (not yet having perfected his aim).

His understanding of the term 'world affairs' surely could not mean that everyone in the whole wide world was at it. He thought that he should ask one of the folks who followed him all the time.

Then he was hit with an unusual rare stunning bout of clarity; and this really affected him.

What he should really concentrate on should be 'terists' and forget world affairs, he thought silently to himself, half enjoying the action of the man in the suit shaking his willy for him before he was zipped up again.

Yes. Terists it would be. Only lately he had received a letter from an Irishman accusing him of being cross-eyed. George decided to add Ireland to the mounting list of evil axis countries then perhaps France, feck them and their Eiffel Tower and funny accents. George was on a roll.

After figuring out where Europe was, George found out that that place contained both Ireland and France and decided that he would not spare the horses and include some other countries as well, close to a place pronounced 'The Meteranan.'

George spent the next few days studying things called Atlases and discovered that the only safe places in the world (despite its poverty, high crime rate, corruption, drug problems and other related things) was the great U.S. of A.

Two years to the day and after long consultations with his dog, George decided it was time to press the button and do the job.

George's aides watched in suspense as he pressed down lightly on the protrusion.

Afterwards he stood proud with a look of satisfaction on his intelligent face and received a well deserved round of applause from the assembled gathering.

The flushing sound of the cistern signalled to all in the tightly packed bathroom that the President had achieved a goal. He had been able to flush the toilet himself for the first time without any assistance whatsoever.

The assembled then united in voice to sing 'Hail to the Chief' and thanked their gods that there appeared to be some confusion in the ranks of their President's brain.

The President then marched back into the Oval Office followed by the pack of toilet singers, while making sure that they all kept in step.

And the world was a safer place.

Rumpy Pumpy

Dinny Jennings was not a happy man. His wife Almonia was not just giving him the cold shoulder, she had also cut off his supply of rumpy pumpy and this in particular was starting to affect his nerves and make him very fidgety.

It all started just because of a simple remark by him about a rash of pimples spreading across her face and how it would be interesting to see what would happen if he were to join the pimples by drawing links across her face as one might do in the puzzle pages of newspapers.

For some reason, which Dinny could not fathom, his gloriously spotted wife Almonia took umbrage to his drawing lines statement and told him there and then *"no more rumpy pumpy for you my good man, from now on its cold Turkey and you can take it or leave it."*

This all happened weeks earlier and because Dinny really adored his piece of rumpy pumpy, the whole situation was starting to get him down. But being a man of invention and innovation, Dinny decided on a course of action to get his wife back in the mood.

Arriving home one evening, he surprised her with a clutch of dimmer switches so that she would be able to dim the lights and not reveal her facial scars, should she so choose. This course of action appeared to have some little affect because while there was still no rumpy pumpy, she at least smiled at him now and again.

It was on the following week that Dinny clinched it and succeeded in getting things back on track. By contacting a friend in the medical supplies business, he was able to procure a steel pimple squeezer. This gift was to thrill and delight Almonia so much, that she broke down in tears, the water streaming down her face causing most of the pimples to turn angry and sore.

Nevertheless she forgave Dinny and whispered in his ear that *"rumpy pumpy was on the menu again,"* promising him some the very next day.

Sure enough on that very next day Almonia came up with the goods as soon as Dinny entered the house after his long day's toil.

Almonia approached, now smiling and happy asking him if he wanted it in the kitchen or on the dining room table. Dinny much preferred it on the table, Almonia knew that, but she liked to tease him.

Sitting at the table with his jacket removed and sleeves rolled up Dinny was thrilled when Almonia came through from the kitchen carrying a tray which held the largest rumpy pumpy pie he had ever seen.

The ingredients of the pie were known only to Almonia as passed on to her by her late mother and as she would one day pass on the secret to their daughter Cascara.

Dinny cut a large chunk off the steaming pie and put in on his plate, licking his lips - he just loved rumpy pumpy.

Devil A Bit

It was rumoured about the place for some time that the Devil was in town. Some of the more religious organised prayer meetings and blessed themselves on a regular basis hoping to keep the offending creature at bay. Some of the less religious prayed silently and blessed themselves in a surreptitious way. Children were warned at school to be on the lookout for a dark faced man dressed in red displaying horns and cloven feet.

Rumour fuelled rumour and there were reported sightings of Satan in such places as Big Eddies Fast Food Emporium, dancing the foxtrot at an afternoon tea dance and driving a pizza delivery motorcycle (it was claimed the pizza's were still hot). Accusing fingers were also pointed at the local bank manager, a Mister Andrew Dalton who was forced to remove his shoes by a group of vigilantes to display his smelly uncloven feet to all of the townspeople. He of course was found to be some bit human but was strongly admonished and ordered to wash his feet.

The astonishing first concrete evidence of the elusive one was to be on a Saturday night at around ten o'clock in Dinny Hogan's Bar. The pub was fairly packed with some people standing at the bar counter, others sitting at the little circular tables scattered around the large lounge. The general mood of the throng was sparkling laughter, good cheer abounding.

The person dressed in a red cloak with two shiny horns jutting out from his head wearing a dark beard which failed to conceal a horrible, pockmarked evil face entered the swing doors of the bar and made his way to the counter as best he could. The cloven feet slipping now and again on the slippery beer covered tiled floor. The barman took the devil's order, *"a gin and tonic, no ice, thank you."*
Satan stood there at the counter and surveyed the crowd, nodding and smiling as if trying to ingratiate himself. Nobody looked at him for fear of catching his eye. All conversation had ceased. The crowd were now numb with fear and dread. The devil stood there alone, in

the packed bar wondering just what he had done to deserve this mass rejection.

The costume! The costume! That was it. He should have known! When Harry O'Hagan had received the invitation to the fancy dress party his first choice of costume was, had to be, that of the devil, what with all the silly rumours abounding. The twits really believed that he was the devil! Harry decided to act it up and on finishing the last of his gin and tonic slowly made his way to the door while letting out a couple of blood curdling screams. The crowd shook in terror, all except one respectable looking old elderly gentleman by the name of Rodney Symms who looked on at all of this with feelings of disgust and revulsion. Rodney finished his half pint and decided to follow the imposter. He went towards the door after Harry O'Hagan.

Rodney would make sure that Harry would suffer for his foolhardiness. It was taking Rodney all of his energy to walk properly. Stuffing size nine cloven hoofs into size ten shoes was no joke. His heels were killing him. Rodney decided to purchase a pair of size eleven shoes tomorrow and also to buy plasters for his sore heels. He caught sight of Harry just a little way ahead of him down the dark street. Rodney followed.

Food for Thought

Alan Grimald was waiting, as usual. He should be used to it by now, but he was not. The years in the business should have toughened him up, but Alan was a softie and found it hard to take the hassle. He checked the equipment. It was in perfect working order. There just never seemed to be enough time.

He was being watched. Out of the corner of his eye, he could see a creature of maybe four feet tall, eyeing him sullenly. Just in front of him there stood a group of four, all different heights animated and excited. He expected that they would be the first to approach him. It could be a long night.

Senta, his wife of twenty years had begged him to give up the business but they both knew that it was too late. When the chips were down, reality had to be faced and the business, dirty as it was, was his profession. It was all he knew. It was all he could do. More of them were gathering. he kept his head down hoping not to be seen, but that of course was pure naivety. They were there, directly in front of him and he could not avoid their stares.

There was a sudden click from the machine and a red warning light flashed. It was time. He slid open the Perspex panel and the crowd surged forward. His well honed intuition proved to be spot on. The group of four led the rest. Money in hand the father of the group gave him his order, *"two hamburgers, two kebabs, four small portions of chips, plenty of tomato ketchup please, oh, and a portion of onion rings."*

The Leprechaun

(A DEEP AND SOMETIMES POIGNANT ANALYSES
OF A PART OF IRISH CULTURE)

As a child Peter O'Sullivan had, of course, heard tales of the leprechaun. He had been told yarns and read of ghosts and goblins and general fairy stories, but they were from a different era, that was all in the past. Now it was MTV, the Internet, and very interesting wars of a clinical nature where no one ever seemed to die. One could safely watch mass bombardments on the news and then switch to 'Married With Children,' without noticing much of a difference.

Peter tried hard to succeed to match the changing times, even changing his drinking habits. Instead of pints of black stout he drank fizzy lager, vodka and coke, the occasional Pernod, sometimes even tequila. He always carried his mobile phone. This was the modern time and Peter was the modern man. He was successful enough in his business endeavours and was quite well off, but things were not happening fast enough. He was constantly dreaming of more wealth and power and impatient for total success. Little did he know it, but his luck was soon to change.

A peculiar happening took place late one Saturday afternoon. While driving back from the races, Peter decided to avoid the heavy traffic and turned off the motorway onto a country lane. Observing the greenery with some distaste, he turned up the music on the car radio to drown out the sound of birds, who were patently trying to outdo each other with their stupid whistling sounds. Glancing to his right he viewed the ever growing volumes of traffic on the road he had just left. He had made the right decision. His was the only vehicle on the narrow laneway. While other drivers would curse and rage on the motorway, Peter would make good time, for time was all important to him, time was money, and money was everything in this modern world. The motorway traffic had slowed to a crawl. He recognized the black Mercedes driven by his friend the politician, who was accompanied by a blond who appeared to be busily engaged in fiddling with the gear lever or something of that nature. Peter slowed down and tried unsuccessfully to catch their attention, but for that action he would have missed the tiny man dressed entirely in green: green hat, green shirt and tie, green jacket, green breeches and stockings to match, and shiny buckled shoes, sitting on a little tree stump hammering little nails into a little shoe.

Peter stopped the car and watched through the rear-view mirror. The little man did not appear to notice him or the car. Alighting from the vehicle he stood and looked back to get a better view. Childhood beliefs and dreams sprang loose from his mind, but this was impossible, leprachauns did not exist, did they, did they? He heard a humming musical sound emanating from the little man, Irish jig music, pleasant enough but certainly not Eurovision material. Peter O'Sullivan thought hard and quickly, reaching that part of his brain which contained the information he needed. Then he remembered that you grab the leprachaun, looking him straight in the eye, if you loosen your grip or take your eyes away he disappears and you do not get your three wishes. (Do I believe in all of this? Do you believe all of this? dear reader, well believe you me, the story as described is true.)

Anyway Peter left the car and proceeded on tippy toes towards his prey, who, obviously possessing an eclectic repertoire had changed his tune to Elvis Presley's 'Love Me Tender.' Just as he was about to start the third line of the chorus, the leprachaun was grabbed vicelike around his little neck by Peter's large hands, but being a trouper, he managed to get as far as the second word of the fourth line of the chorus.

Peter shouted out, almost hysterically. *"Caught you, you little green fucker, now give me my three wishes, or you are a dead fairy."* The little green man croaked in response, *"I am not a fairy, I am a straight leprachaun interfering with nobody, now piss off and leave me alone."* The grip on his neck tightened and Peter threatened *"three shaggin' wishes and do not try to distract me or you are a dead leprachaun."* The leprechaun, being both very old and very wise and possessing a strong fear of death, decided to acquiesce and play the game. Better to play the game despite the unfair rules, then not be allowed play at all and be permanently dropped. *"Name your three wishes,"* he croaked.

Peter, with slow intonation, recited his wishes. *"Okay. First, I want to be the best looking man in the world. Second, I want to live in the biggest house in the land. Third I want to be the most fabulously wealthy and well-known person in the world. Now do your stuff or I will press your little chicken neck to shit."* The leprechaun knew that he was well and truly snookered (I mean, two requests in the last wish! That was abusing the whole thing). Nevertheless he nodded his head and gargled the magic words, *"let it be"* (yes, from his repertoire).

The now extremely handsome and perfect Peter was immediately transported to the country's largest building, the National Prison, where he was the object of much admiration, desire, and attention from both prisoners and wardens alike. They found him both magnetic and attractive. He really did not seem to fit the different descriptions and titles bestowed on him by the mass media, the most quoted being 'The Biggest Serial Killer Ever,' being credited with the murders of five hundred and seventy five men, women, and children, all killed by strangulation. It was said that he would have been caught earlier, but for using some of his vast wealth to bribe his way along.

On the day in court, after he was kicked, spat on, and felt up, he was sentenced to ninety-nine years in prison, and then to be executed. Peter entered The Guinness Book of Records on three counts:

(1)   He was the most gorgeous prisoner ever.
(2)   He had committed the greatest number of murders ever by one individual.
(3)   He was the wealthiest prisoner ever on death row.

This is the end of this simple but true story and if it has a moral, the moral surely is, if you see any little man dressed in green, walk on by, or you could finish up in serious trouble in many ways and finish up with too much time on your hands, or too little.

Outcome

Of course Frankie Downey believed in fairies! Don't we all! Well not anymore really. In the days of homes of flickering lights it was a lot easier to conjure up ghosts, hobgoblins, and fairies. Then the change to electricity brought brightness to the dark corners, and the shadows shrunk and disappeared.

Single, and in his late thirties, Frankie was strongly influenced as a child by his mother's reading to him of tales of the Brothers Grimm and Hans Christian Anderson. Whilst some of the tales raised the hairs on his nape, he enjoyed most of them and was still influenced and imbued with the whole idea and make believe of a place of wonder, a special magical place hidden out there. A place for him.

Frankie would still sometimes pursue his interest, buying books on leprechauns, elves, and other things of a supernatural nature. He did not discuss this with any of his friends. He did not wish to be considered odd.

Frankie was convinced that the large circular mound near his little cottage was a Fairy Fort. He thought he heard music on a number of occasions but whenever he got close, the music halted and all there was left was silence. But he knew - he could feel it.

The death of his mother left Frankie feeling desolate, sad, and very much alone. He sat in the house wondering about his life and what would become of him.

The morning had started off alright, the sun was watery, but the forecast was for fine weather and while there was cloud, Frankie felt that it was flying too high to be of any immediate danger.

Anyway he needed to get out of the house, to get away from the place which still held his mother's presence. It did not feel like his house anymore. It was most peculiar. It was as if the house had changed or maybe it was Frankie himself. He was not sure.

Deciding to walk through the fields had seemed like a good idea until the fog came. First in patches, leaving occasional doorways for Frankie to walk through, then thickening to such an extent that Frankie's vision was totally affected and he slowed his pace to a crawl, having absolutely no idea of his direction.

Was he imagining it? He must be! No, it was music, it was distant but it was music. The Fairy Fort! He must be near the Fairy Fort. The sound appeared to be coming from the right, turning slightly Frankie walked slowly in that direction. The fog was lifting, but in its own time. Frankie saw some recognisable signs. He was nearing the Fairy Fort, only this time, instead of halting, the music was increasing in volume.

The swirling vapour had lifted enough to give him a clear view of the fort. He was in a clearing containing his magical musical mound but otherwise surrounded by a wall of apparently solid vapour. Then he watched as the sliding grass-covered door opened to allow him to slowly make his way through.

As the door slid shut the noisy din impacted on him. He had expected sweetness and light in this place. Instead it was packed with leather clad individuals, some dancing, others just lounging at the bar drinking!

Frankie got near the bar after some considerable shoving and pushing. A beer was pushed in his direction without his asking and he sipped from the glass while reading the text on the large banner strung across from wall to wall. It said 'Gay Rights.' 'We Demand Equality.'
Frankie had found his Fairy Fort and all the fairies he wanted. He decided to stay and not go back to the cottage.

Last Call

The Jones family were well known as a family of hard drinkers. Billy, the father of three strapping sons by the names of Tommy, Mikey and Paddy had difficulty being served in most bars because of his troublesome ways. The family always ended up back at the bar owned by Bull McCarthy, who was known to serve anyone with cash in hand.

Bull McCarthy was known as a man with nerves of steel who could be seen to hop over the counter in a rage whenever an affray started and would knock drunken heads together before slinging the offenders out through the door and onto the street. 'The Bull' as he was called always demanded money up front before filling a drink.

Annie McCarthy, the wife of Billy and mother of the three younger sons, would join the rest of the family on one or two nights in the week at 'The Bull's,' but, much preferred to drink at home - snapping the tops off the cans of high alcohol volume cider as she sat watching her favourite soaps on television, often shedding a tear of sympathy whenever some misfortune would overcome one of her favourite characters.

It was on a Thursday night after being refused in a few of the more respectable establishments and causing a fracas on refusal that the whole family returned to the Bull's to indulge in a lot of drink and then more, that it happened.

There was a family rule that each member of the clan called for their own drink, so as to avoid confusion later on as to whose round it was. Billy, who suspected everyone, especially his own family of avoiding a round and taking advantage of his good nature when he was under the weather, had introduced this rule.
Billy was standing at the bar counter watching the pint of stout as it slowly settled when he felt a sharp pain in his chest. Lifting his hand he rubbed his chest rigorously in an attempt to rid himself of the worsening ache. The last thing he saw were the hands of The Bull

finishing off what looked like a perfect pint, topped by a lovely creamy head, before he dropped to the floor, dying of a massive heart attack.

There was much excitement and pandemonium in the bar as the crowd surged forward vying with each other in speculation and guesswork as to 'is he dead or not.' The Bull did his usual hop over the counter, shoving the customers aside to lift Billy's hand and feel his pulse. The Bull announced to the punters that Billy was definitely dead.

Billy's family observed all this from the edge of the now silent throng. They slowly advanced through the gap made by the respectful crowd and walked towards the body.

The deceased lay on his left side and was facing them, his eyes still open with a look of torture on his face. They advanced again to within a foot of the departed and looked at each other, disbelief showing on their faces.

As one, they surged forward each attempting to grab the now well settled pint but only succeeding in knocking it over and spilling it along the bar top.

Silence broke out again, but only for a very short time. The family tore into each other, each blaming the other for causing the dreadful waste of such a lovely pint. The mother was the first to strike out, then the whole family indulged in battering each other.

The Bull eventually succeeded in separating them, asking them to show some respect for the dead and the waste of a good pint. The family eventually retired back to their seats cursing their misfortune on the loss of such a perfect pint, and of course, a father.

The History of Blisters

Biggley Eddibody thought up the title long before he added the story to suit it. He thought that the title 'The History of Blisters' would have a certain snob appeal.

He expected the first steps to be fairly straight forward and simple but it was not so. After waiting in his doctor's surgery for well over an hour, he was quickly ejected from the premises, the doctor being very quick to discover that his request for a prescription and literature on anything to do with blisters was based on the totally bogus claim by Biggley that he had cultivated a blister under the big toe of his left foot. On examination, all the good doctor could find was a flawless, slightly smelly foot. The doctor accused Biggley of being an impostor and after calling in his receptionist they both threw Biggley onto the street outside after first searching him and extracting the medical fee plus a tip.

On arriving at his local library he immediately went to the research section and looked under 'Blisters,' there was nothing! There were books and extremely informative magazines pieces on bunions, warts, freckles, ingrown toenails, nail-biting, spitting, flatulence, taxidermy, Do It Yourself Dentistry, dirty dancing, creating the perfect omelette and such sundry gripping information, but as to anything relating to blisters, Biggley's search produced zilch. His agile mind soon came up with (what to him) was a superb solution. He decided to grow his own, and fully and properly research the blistering question of blisters, so there!

Biggley decided to switch from a size nine shoe to a size eight in an attempt to emulate a genuine blister carrier and after some weeks of non-success, changed down again to a size seven. Except for causing some bleeding to his toes, pinching the skin from his heels and causing him to adopt a most peculiar pose as if he were carrying something in his pants, there was no change in Biggley's condition.

Biggley took to the street under the guise of a market researcher and after some general questions, he would try and slip in a question on blisters. This pathetic attempt produced furious rows with people complaining at this monstrous invasion of privacy. He learned nothing.

Biggley tried sitting outside confessional boxes at churches hoping to hear someone mention the word 'blister.' All he acquired was the knowledge that there were many sinners in this world, murderers, fornicators, sexual deviants and others, and that was only the priests! His efforts came to nought. He decided to reduce his shoe size again.

This is the last and tragically sad chapter on the vagaries of Biggley Eddibody and his quest to find, investigate and write about the scourge of the blister. After reducing shoe sizes again and again his suffering feet could face no more and giving one last gasp on the sight of a size four they collapsed on the floor, bringing Biggley with them, dying from foot strangulation (self inflicted).

It would be so easy for any of us to criticise Biggley for the cruel treatment of his feet, but what he did, he did for science and the advancement of mankind and feet all over the world. Let us unite in tribute to the man of the century, Bibbley Eddibody, a name to be remembered. R.I.P.

The Halistosis Kid

Umbreto Livia was an amazing man. The only son of the Livia banking family, he was often seen to grace the society pages of some of the more duff papers. A snapshot here on a yacht, a photo there at the races, but whatever and whenever the captured event Umbreto was always to be seen in the company of a different woman.He was never, never, with the same woman twice. This was a phenomenon often remarked upon in the pages of some of the self same newspapers.

It could be said that Umbreto was no spring chicken, in fact he was due soon at the gate marked number forty and his loving parents were getting kind of worried that he showed no inclination towards marriage - but little did they know.

His father Ilbred and mother Constance had met at a home for rejected children when they were both at the age of twenty and discovered that they each possessed an insatiable desire for money. This acted as a cheap aphrodisiac and provided many years of fun for the pair. They went from selling newspaper to retailing and from that to banking, causing the odd suicide along the way, but the fortune grew and the fun went on.

Umbreto pondered and wondered. He just could not figure it out, for whatever reason women did not stay with him very long. In fact, women did not stay with him at all. Since his tender years, women refused to go out with him. The beauties gracing the newspapers with him were all paid companions. Some were hookers, some were not, but for some strange reason all refused to go out with him a second time, even rejecting double pay. Umbreto looked at himself in the mirror and saw a fairly plump but agreeable looking man, with all of his own teeth and hair and wearing clothing of a conservative, but expensive nature.
Sheila Delap was a kind and feisty soul, generous of nature and totally honest. Any other woman would have let her hair grow to help cover the enormous flaps which are normally called ears, but that was

31

not Sheila. *"Take me as you find me"* was her motto. Pity was, few wanted to find her, let alone take her.

Umbreto was at crisis point, his written invitation to attend the International Bankers Ball (which included the logo of a screw), said *"Mr. Umbreto Livia and friend are invited to attend the Annual Ball to be held this year at the Palace of Idiots"* (Government House). Umbreto had no partner. He rang around in desperation but to no avail. There was not a woman who would attend the ball with him. He looked in the mirror again to reassure himself. Was it something he had said?

The little car being driven along the busy streets was ageing and starting to show it. Sheila shoved her dainty foot down harder on the accelerator but it made little or no impression. The car was on its last legs.

The Porsche being driven by Umbreto was being held back by a silly little car in front. He blew his horn furiously, only to receive a two fingered salute from the driver ahead. In his anxiety to pass out the car driven by Sheila, he pressed harder on his accelerator only to strike the car of Sheila Delap in the rear, causing her to swerve and hit a pole.

Umbreto quickly halted and jumped from his car, regret showing on his fat face. He opened the driver's door of the little car to be met by the owner of the biggest pair of ears he had ever seen. Not withstanding, he proceeded to catch her by the neck and attempted to help her out of the car. She fainted in his arms and he immediately rang for an ambulance.

The doctor approached him in the hospital hallway still wearing his mask. On enquiring Umbreto was informed that Sheila Delap (he now knew her name) was in good health and ready to go home. He peered through the window marked 'Casualty' and saw her again. She was not the greatest looker, but she did have the biggest ears he ever saw and he found this very attractive.

In the hospital, as in all other places, Umbreto had a space all to himself. This he put down to his family name and the respect shown for it. He watched as Sheila left casualty and walk towards the exit, her ears flapping in a most attractive way. He hastened after her, to introduce himself and to apologise for his stupidity on the road. He caught her just as she was about to enter the lift. Tapping her on the shoulder, he quickly explained all about the accident being his fault and offering her transportation to her destination.

Sheila Delap looked him straight in the eyes and asked: *"Do you know that you suffer from a thing called halitosis?"*

Umbreto was stunned. No. Umbreto was knocked out. No. Umbreto was utterly flabbergasted. No, Umbreto was to witness his life flash before him and saw and recollected all the rejections down through the years. NOW he understood, and it was all thanks to Sheila with the big ears.

They attended the ball and enjoyed it immensely, drawing much attention from the crowd. They danced every dance, her ears flapping widely, his face covered with a surgeon's mask.

It was discovered that his type of halitosis was incurable, so he was to wear a mask for the rest of his days (not the same mask of course). They were destined to wed, and produced four children, two boys and two girls, all with foul smelling breath and very big ears, but they were very rich, so it did not really matter. The grandparents Ilbred and Constance were thrilled with the change in Umbreto and that the family name of Livia would live on. And Sheila's ears? They lived flappily ever after. (I know, I know, but it's late and I am tired)!!!

A Fairy Tale

Once upon a time there lived a very wily king by the name of Luka. Luka knew the score. As king, he did not just observe rules, he made them. He was the richest man in the land. His great great great great great great great great great greatgrandfather Elbow the Nudge, was the very first king of the land and possessed all that anybody needed to know to become king. Large in stature, bulky by nature and having no conscience whatsoever, he engaged in the slaughter and eviction of peasants, forcing them to rent back their own hovels from him. For that time predated banks, so they could not borrow money to buy back their own home, (that particular scam was thought up many years later by one of his descendants). Anyway, they either paid him or suffered the sword. Out of his evergrowing cache, he built himself a large castle and proclaimed himself king over all others who would henceforth be known as 'subjects.' Over time the peasantry began to accept this situation as normal and life settled. They even grew to love and admire him, particularly after his many banquets when he would send out the leftovers to be distributed among them. Elbow the Nudge perceived acts of charity were noted by the church authorities and canonisation would be seriously discussed following his demise.

Anyway, King Luka was blessed with only one child of the female variety but Luka had to make do. She was a beautiful girl by the name of Luscious, who, because of the death of his wife Divine, took up a lot of his time. To make sure that she stayed pure, he had her watched very carefully. All of her trips outside the castle gates were carefully monitored. She would be accompanied by a coterie of ladies in waiting and a dozen burly soldiers who would beat a path through the adoring crowds, for King Luka did not like his precious Luscious mixing with the rabble, particularly those who were not female. To find her the right kind of husband he had just in fact, sent out a message to all of the ruling houses in the neighbouring kingdoms, proposing union through the marriage of his lovely daughter to one of their princely sons. There was an accompanying note, signed by the court physician, verifying that she was intact. In those days, dear reader, there was much interbreeding between the ruling royals, but you surely understand the king's logic in trying to keep it in the family - after all, the devil you know is likely to be better than a stranger, or so the old adage goes...

Theatre work was hard. It was even harder when you could not get it. Errol Palmer's last gig was working as the rear end of a donkey in a revue at the Alpha Theatre, where the alcohol sozzled mob pelted the stage with rotten fruit and vegetables. After rescuing some of the missiles for future consumption, Errol beat a hasty retreat just before the drunken crowd invaded the stage and tore the seats to pieces. This part of the show was much appreciated by the remaining audience, who stamped their feet clapped and cheered, while breaking up the wooden benches.

Errol found the notice pinned to the wall of the tavern, 'MINSTREL WANTED, FED AND FOUND, APPLY CASTLE GATES - NO TIME WASTERS.' Errol was not a bad looking fellow, not particularly good looking either, but as a thespian he could well project an image. He loved showbiz, and the world was his stage, (the world was flat at that time, by the way). He decided to go to the castle on that very same day and attend for an interview.

After being checked and searched at the large gate he was escorted to the main hall where sat King Luka and Princess Luscious. The king roared out *"NOW, SHOW ME WHAT YOU CAN DO."* Errol produced a jewsharp from under his green feathered cap and proceeded to play a lively tune. After some minutes, the king raised his hand aloft, and shouted *"anything else?"* Errol then danced while still playing the jewsharp, *"anything else?"*, again shouted the king. Errol proceeded to sing a ballad while still dancing and playing the jewsharp. Again the king shouted "STOP," dismissing Errol and had him escorted to the hallway outside to wait.

King Luka, ever conscious of Luscious's vulnerability to those of the male persuasion, asked the opinion of his daughter regarding Errol. *"Well what do you think, Luscious my dear?"* Luscious knew full well that if she gave the nod, Errol would not get the job, and she had found him quite amusing. *"No Father, interview some more,"* she responded. By that very act, she ensured that Errol Palmer secured the position of court minstrel. It was to prove to be a fateful action on her part. Errol for his part had succeeded in not staring too hard at lavish Luscious while doing his act. Errol valued his head and all other attachments.

It proved to be an easy life at the castle, three or four gigs a week and all the food he could eat. In his spare time he honed and developed his art. There was one little worry, and that was the strong sexual attraction he felt for Luscious. Luscious for her part treated him as she would any other underling. Errol Palmer resolved to get Luscious into bed and he bided his time. He was formulating a plan of action. Errol was a patient man.

Luscious began to trust Errol somewhat. He dogged her at all times and became her lapdog. Any need and he was at her disposal. Any errand and he ran. If she showed the slightest sign of a cold, he was to be seen collecting the appropriate herbs to help ease her. But for all his attention she still kept her royal distance.

During his reconnoitring of the castle, he discovered one very interesting fact. The king was an extraordinary heavy sleeper. In order to put this newly gained knowledge to the test, Errol once pushed over a suit of armour situated just outside the king's chamber. He ran quickly from the scene but soon returned to help others to put it back on its feet. While nobody was looking, he peeped in through the door of the king's chamber - the king was sleeping like a baby.

Errol planned it well. During a banquet, he made sure that the goblets of both King Luka and Princess Luscious were kept full, plying them with triple x mead. The drunken king grunted in satisfaction, thinking that he had made a wise choice in entertainers. What did women know?

Princess Luscious' bed chamber was but a short distance from her father's. After carefully walking the corridor a number of times and testing the alertness of the sentry by hitting him on the head with a large cudgel, Errol felt secure enough to knock on the door of Princess Luscious. He went in on hearing an imperious 'ENTER.' She looked at him aghast and was about to shower him with drunken insults for entering her chamber when he said *"Your father."* *"What?"* *"Your father sent me to fetch you, it's urgent."* Scrambling from her bed she ran ahead of him to her father's room. The room was almost in darkness, lit only by a small candle on the far window ledge. *"What ails you, Father, what ails you?"* Her father's voice growled out, *"I am not ailing, but I have watched and observed and I have grown to like and respect Errol, he is the son I never had, I want Errol to become family, I want you to wed him."* She turned to look at Errol but could barely see him in the darkness. Her father's voice boomed out gain, *"Now go, take him to your chamber and enjoy."* She had always obeyed her father, but this! To be expected to cavort with one of the lowly help. It was asking rather a lot. *"Are you sure Father, are you sure?"* *"Of course I am sure, now I command you to take him to your chamber."* She duly did.

Errol and Luscious had a wonderful night, Errol taking advantage of her many times. Galloping away from the castle in the early hours, he thanked his lucky stars for his talents. His early training and much practise as a ventriloquist and impressionist had finally paid off, giving him the gig of a lifetime.

AND THEY ALL LIVED HAPPILY EVER AFTER.

Timetable

He sat comfortably in his seat, putting his foot down at first on the accelerator, giving it a gentle revving, just to test its power and get the feel of the engine. Testing to make sure that the mechanics had done their job properly. To win this race today was important to him in his career and the fewer pit stops the better. As a driver with a reputation, he was determined to stay at number one. Glancing slyly at the competition he saw No. 52 on his right, but he would be easily beaten. The others were also not in his class. His only danger was from No. 12 who was as ruthless as himself, but he had beaten him in the past and would do it again. He had nerves of steel and experience to boot. He also had the killer instinct and knew that fear was something one had to feel, understand, and control. He was already experiencing the thrill of racing past the finishing line to the cheers of the crowd. He looked at his watch - it was nearly time. The chequered flag went up.

People jumped from the roadway as the line of buses tore past them. Competition was the spice of life and all that, but this new bus speeding epidemic was ridiculous.

'Interview with a Politician'

"I'm glad you asked me that question. The response of any of my fellow ministers to all questions of that nature has been solid and unequivocal. We, the government, are well aware of situations developing on an on-and-off going basis, and are working in unity to find an acceptable solution. We are, at the present time, examining the whole complex business and indeed after looking at and talking to the people at the coalface, who are the experts in their own field, we have concluded that while the infrastructure is sound, we have to accept that there is a lot of work to be done on the ground. However, we refuse to be bullied or intimidated by self-seeking individuals or pressure groups. In addition, you must appreciate that the government is already under tremendous stress from groups representing old age pensioners and other subversives. I would remind the electorate that only for pensioners and sick people we would be in a position to lower taxes substantially. This is something that the opposition parties and some media people conveniently ignore. I hope that my response is to your satisfaction. I must now conclude, as I leave to head a fact finding delegation investigating the growth of tourism and bananas in the Canary Islands. I must now leave you sir."

Questioner: *"But I only asked you the right time!"*

Keeping up with the Jones

Ken's job at the bank secured him a certain standing in the community. His salary was more than adequate to maintain a lifestyle in relation to his position as assistant manager. The problem was that both Ken and his wife Martina lived well beyond their means. Membership of the golf clubs, the expensive private boarding schools for their three children, the expenses required in running two cars and the rather large house with expensive well-manicured lawn and gardens ate into their finances.

Despite all of this, they holidayed abroad every year, returning home to regale their friends with tales of expensive exotic travels in far away places. The friends would be duly impressed, sighing with envy and marvelling at the deep tans displayed by the couple.

But Ken and Martina Ball had a dark secret and shame and pride ensured that it remained a secret. Their descriptions of their travels were in fact gained through reading of upmarket travel brochures picked up at the more exclusive travel agents. They would wait and seek out cheap package holiday cancellations, and book at the last minute at much reduced prices making sure to wear the darkest of sunglasses to avoid any possible recognition.

The plane was full of jolly holiday makers. Ken and Martina sat in their seats, again scanning the crowd anxious that they might see a face they knew. The coast appeared to be clear. They removed their sunglass disguises and relaxed.

The beach was littered with people in various states of undress - the oiled and factored bodies glistening in the sun. Ken and Martina eventually found a stony spot at the far end of the beach which was less crowded and after making sure of their security they spread out their towels and lay back to engage with the sun's rays.

Always avoiding the popular eateries, they would walk and walk until they would find a quiet, out of the way, place which would not

40

be attended by the lower classes and usually was cheaper. It was Martina who first spotted the chalk written sign on the lopsided blackboard, 'Eat as much as you can,' 'Two for the price of one.' They entered the small Russian restaurant and looked around. Empty of people, it contained six tables, each covered by wax tablecloths in need of cleaning. The floor was greasy with signs of pieces of food left by previous diners. Well, what the hell, it was cheap, two for the price of one was good value at any cost. A shabbily dressed little lady appeared from behind a beaded curtain and advanced towards them. She opened her mouth to reveal dark spaces between her cracked yellow teeth. Gesturing towards a table, she said, *"Sit, sit."* They sat and were rewarded with a small single sheet of paper headed by the word 'Menu.' They could not make head or tail of the strange Russian writing and called to their host, looking for help. Smiling she pointed at an item on the menu, repeating *"special, special,"* in a thick guttural voice. They nodded their heads in acceptance and she left through the beaded curtains after grabbing the piece of paper from them. They shook their heads and pursed their lips at this display of ill manners and ignorance.

Bread appeared. Well, it looked like bread, but it was nearly black and it was hard. Then followed the main course. Two large bowls of a cold stew-like dish containing whole unpeeled potatoes, a dark kind of meat set in a sort of cabbage gravy obviously thickened with flour and separate plates of vegetables which had remained uncooked. Some were still covered with earth.

It took time, but Ken and Martina persevered and finished most of it, despite feeling a little queasy. To avoid leaving a tip or any payment at all they were to be seen exiting very fast and legging it up the side street, being chased by the little old lady.

Their standing in the community took a battering after their Russian restaurant activities were shown on the television show with the highest ratings 'Candid Cameos.' People laughed and laughed at the mean antics of the pretentious couple.

After that, very few asked them where they went on their holidays. Everyone knew!

The Rat Pack

Does self-preservation give birth to greed, or is greed an organic in-built weapon in step with self-preservation. Take the case of Amanda Grey. Amanda was one of the wealthy Grey family much revered by certain sections of the media who equated wealth with breeding, but then there is no accounting for taste or balance.

Amanda was the brittle offspring of the Hon. Marcus and Elizabeth Grey whose country estate was large enough to have most of it rented out to farmers willing to pay, and some of the rest for hunting and shooting. While the Greys were wily, they were also very much aware of the need to avoid hard work in any shape or form, being well aware that hard work killed many a man.

Anyway, back to the lovely Amanda. At the age of thirty-four she already had three marriages behind her. The first husband had drowned in suspicious circumstances in the bath. But membership of the lodge ensured that the inquest result was 'Accidental death by inhalation of water.' The second was lost overboard from a ferry plying its trade between Dover and Calais, the remains of bits of a body were found at different stages in the straits. The consensus was that the body was unlucky in that it had got caught up in the propellers of at least three different ships. Hence the lack of any remaining body parts of any decent size. He was finally identified by an initialled wedding ring found on a finger in the belly of a mackerel fished up by two priests out for a days angling, who were really surprised when they got the finger from a fish. The third husband was found much flattened after being dropped from a plane somewhere in the vicinity of Las Vegas. The coroner stated that he probably died of fear before his assault on the ground.

Each one of Amanda'a husbands was wealthy in his own right, their unfortunate deaths being the cause of adding to the wealth and riches of the Grey family through natural inheritance and large insurance policy payouts. The Grey family crest contained the motto' Life is what you make it.' In the case of the Greys the opposite was probably more suitable.

The hunting party stopped in front of the Country Inn, all bedecked in red and black, buckles, bugles and excitedly mad hounds, all out for the kill. The Greys owned all the land surrounding and also the land the pub stood on, so the pre-hunt drinkies would be free for all or the publican would find himself slung out on his ear. The crowd dismounted from their horses and went to indulge themselves at the Country Inn, allowing themselves to be led in by the Hon. Marcus Grey, his strapping wife Elizabeth, and their lovely (thrice) widowed daughter Amanda.

The landlord Ben Briston, who was well used to the intrusive and mean nature of the Greys, said, *"What will it be?"*, with a look of stoic resignation on his face. His recently hired barman was needed so he shouted loudly down to the cellar, *"Rock, get up here fast."* A voice boomed back, *"Coming boss."*

The dark swarthy looks of the tall well-built Rock would have knocked Amanda off her saddle if she had been sitting on it. He opened his handsome mouth to ask *"What will it be folks?"*, while displaying a set of glistening white teeth equalled in beauty only by his mop of jet black hair set in a kind of tousled shoulder length way. Amanda could not speak. She was incapable of anything except love. So this must be what love is?

Hurriedly leaving the Inn, for fear of swooning and dropping her monacle in the process, she was soon outside just in time to see a fox trotting by and stopping to urinate just feet from the tied up howling pack of dogs.

She watched as the fox casually continued his journey. The dogs were livid by now, frothing and straining at their leashes. After some time, she did not know how long, she decided to release the dogs to get the fox, as an act or charity. She thought, *"Is this me? Being charitable?"* Just then the fox appeared again, this time running somewhat faster as a result of being chased by the pack of mad dogs. She ran to block his path but he dodged her and ran straight into the Inn, followed by the pack.

44

Amanda could hear the bedlam, shouting, swearing, and cursing coming from the inside of the Inn, but decided to wait and compose herself some more before entering. There were roars of urgent persuasion from the Inn crowd. Then there was silence.

The dogs came out in mini packs of twos and threes, some boasting bloody jowls. She was happy for them, they had their kill. Marcus and Elizabeth were the first of the crowd to appear, their faces flushed with excitement and drink. *"Best kill I ever witnessed,"* Marcus enthused. Elizabeth agreed, knocking back the last of her drink. The rest of the crowd followed, their faces filled with animation.

Marcus stood up on the stirrups of his horse and asked the gathering, *"What say we get another one?"* The crowd roared approval and all went towards their mounts chattering happily.

Amanda cursed herself for missing all the excitement, and cursed herself for her sudden unexplained act of charity. She decided to have a quick look in the bar. She had not noticed the tail, but she was sure nobody had claimed the trophy. Maybe she could.

On entering through the door she was to witness a bar awash with bits of skin, bones and sticky blood. She asked Ben Briston *"Where's the fox?"* Ben shrugged his shoulder, *"He got away, the dogs went for Rock instead."*

This news was quite upsetting for Amanda until she spotted a mop of bloody black hair on the floor. She grabbed it fast in case somebody else would return and claim it. Holding it aloft she examined it. It was a mighty mane. She wouldn't go home empty-handed.

Exceptions

Chicken Johnny was aptly nicknamed - shy, gentle and peaceful he was, and heroics were not his forte, for Johnny was a reliable and recognisable coward. His peers had long since stopped debating and questioning his inability to suffer any kind of hassle. Accepting him for what he was - a base, un-heroic wimp.

Cowardice was a family trait. His mother was a coward, as was his father, and indeed all of his four sisters. Many's the time Johnny would make it to his house heavily scarred, having failed to outrun an attacker. It was not that Johnny would refuse to fight back, it was just that he did not know how, so I suppose it was a mixture of obscurantism and stupidity. The trips outside of the house were getting less frequent for our cowardly friend as the attacks increased and so did the marks and scars on his face and body.

This situation lasted for quite a number of years until his face became so marked as to become so ugly and unrecognisable that his family stopped talking to him and refused to let him into the house anymore. His four sisters complained that with his ugly puss around the place, they were finding it very hard to get suitors. I mean, think about it. Four very shy sisters and one ugly marked brother. On his thirtieth birthday to the day, Chicken Johnny clucked no more, dying from exposure and lack of balls and good looks.

There is no moral to this story, but if there was one, it surely would be, 'try to be born brave and handsome and you might be in this place a little longer.' That is, if you want to.

Swinging Time

Amsterdam is a wonderful city, seeming to cater for all tastes, with its large selection of stylish buildings, museums, canals for swimmers and suicides, and murders, coffee shops selling weed filled chocolate and cakes as well as the weed itself, brothels, windows sporting women of all persuasions, Asian, black, white, fat, thin, tall, small, a minority even exhibiting fabulous moustaches filling the windows of the streets in the red light district with a sense of that commercial comprehension for which the Dutch are renowned.

It was, I think, on the second day of our visit that after perusing our map we found that by taking a shortcut through the university grounds, we could save ourselves some time. To get to the university, we, of course, had to cross one of the many bridges straddling the neat canals. Bridges shaped like rows of metal people stuck in the up position of the push-up exercise.

As we turned the corner to the right at the bridge and headed towards the university, we could not help but observe the pretty woman sitting on the long bench facing the canal. What interested and intrigued us completely was the fact that in her right hand she held a banana between her forefinger and thumb and was seen to swing it around whenever anyone approached.

When it was our turn, she smiled at us and swung the banana. We walked along but at my insistence we stopped to view this most unusual of spectacles. After some minutes, I suggested that we return to her and ask her why she was a banana swinger and to what purpose. My partner reluctantly agreed and trooped back to the bench where she sat.

I was very polite. *"Excuse me,"* I said, *"but would you mind telling me why are you swinging the banana?"* She looked at me in surprise and appeared to be a little taken aback at my question.

"It's for a bit of fun, it makes people smile, anyway it's not a banana it's a

banana skin."

I looked down and sure enough she was right, it was just the skin without the flesh. I immediately apologised and started again. *"Excuse me, would you please tell me why you are swinging the banana skin?"* At this she got up from the seat and walked away with a cranky look on her face

I suppose it takes all types to make up a world and that includes a fruit swinging Dutchwoman and a nosey Irishman.

Gravely Serious

Rodney McGuillin planned his own funeral with meticulous detail. He had the eulogy written and ordered the best dark marble headstone that money could buy. He had bought an expensive suit with a matching tie and pocket handkerchief to go with the casket which he was sure would enhance his profile on the day of his demise. The undertaker was paid in cash up front and he had even left enough money with the bar owner just beyond the graveyard so as that his mourners could have a free drink or two in remembrance of him.

The only problem was that he was all done when he was at the age of fifty six and what with a dicky heart, high blood pressure, ingrown toenails and other ailments he had not expected to last at all, but that was all of a few years ago and here he was, still alive and kicking (well, not kicking very hard of course, what with the ingrown toenails) and nary a sign of death in any form whatsoever approaching.

Rodney was very perplexed, frustrated, and annoyed wondering what he should do to solve the upsetting situation. Then he had a brainwave! To hell with death, he would have the funeral while he was still alive. The money was there! The mothballed suit was still hanging up, dated but nevertheless containing good material. All was in place, except a body, but Rodney reasoned "You can't have everything."

Rodney was not able to procure the services of a clergyman - all refused to pray over and bless an empty coffin although some were tempted by the offer of extra cash but resisted on the grounds that people might laugh at them officiating at a bodyless funeral and it could cost them at future collections. The undertaker had no qualms at all in granting Rodney his most unusual request after explaining that, what with inflation and general rising costs, Rodney would have to stump up to keep pace. Rodney understood completely and readily parted with the extra dosh.

The notice duly appeared on the death notices of the next day's newspaper, inviting all interested parties to join Rodney McGuillin at his own funeral and inviting them to join him afterwards, at the bar adjoining the cemetery, for a few drinks.

The offer was taken up by many who knew him and many who did not. Crowds thronged the funeral home to view the empty coffin where stood Rodney, ready to shake the hands of the line of last respectors. Rodney was thrilled with the turnout and promised himself that it was an effort worth considering a repeat.

Rodney had contacted the publican, promising him extra money to cater for the expected large turnout if he would provide soup, sandwiches and things on crackers. The publican was readily agreeable, delighted at the idea of so much extra business. The deal was done.

The multitudes at the graveside were a source of joy and pride to Rodney. With swollen chest, he directed the undertaker and gravediggers as to the proper way to drop down the coffin without damaging either the casket or the side of the freshly dug pit.

As the first pieces of earth hit the coffin from the long shovels of the diggers, Rodney found it very hard to contain his excitement, so hard in fact that his dicky heart started to act up (or down) before stopping completely, causing him to stumble forward slightly and then to fall down into the grave, hitting the coffin with a loud racket.

All of this carry on caused no little excitement, with the remaining crowd deciding to stay on, if only to see if there would be any more unusual occurrences at this most unusual funeral.

The undertaker sized up the situation and decided that there was only one course of action to take. He, the undertaker, was already paid and under the circumstances would be unlikely to be paid again (by this particular client anyway). So after procuring a hoist and attaching hooks to both sides of the coffin, he and his colleagues eventually hauled the box back up from the ground. It was still topped by the now rigor mortised person of Rodney McGuillan, sitting astride the shining brass decorated long container as if he had died riding a horse or a motorcycle.

After some discussion between the undertaker, his men and the gravediggers it was decided that the only civilised thing to do was to throw the body down into the bottom of the grave and then to drop the coffin on top of him, in the hope that it might straighten him out some bit. As soon as they lobbed the coffin back down onto the body and heard some cracking sounds, they knew that their daring and inventive plan had worked. Once again they proceeded to shovel the earth back down onto the coffin, hoping for no more interruptions. There were none.

As soon as the publican heard the news that the deceased was really dead, he stopped serving anymore free drink and retrieved as much of the soup, sandwiches, and things on crackers as he and his staff possibly could, declaring that it was unpaid for and that *"that bollix McGuillin had broken his word."* This outburst caused a lot of resentment and consternation, particularly among those who had not had any drink, soup, or food of any description whatsoever.

A fight broke out in the bar between those who were seen to have signs of food around their mouths and smelled of drink and those who were hungry and sober, so, what had started off as a simple burial plan by a man of vision and generosity, turned into a riot and the police had to be called to quell the disorder.

A sad end indeed to what should have been a wonderful day out and a lovely story. But maybe we can learn something from all of this - although what that something might be, I really don't know - and if there is a moral in here somewhere, I'm damned if I know what it is!

Time Goes By

I'm not really into jewellery but when the hyperactive street vendor stopped me while walking through the dry, dusty streets in Bodrum in Southern Turkey, I must admit to have taken a shine to one watch in his collection, a fake gold Rolex which seemed to stand out from all the other watches. I was easily tempted.

After some friendly haggling we agreed on a price and I immediately removed the leather strap watch from my wrist and exchanged it for my fake gold Rolex with matching gold and fake titanium strap. I thought it looked very well.

Some three years later I holidayed in Tenerife in Las Cristianos, an area known to be popular with people of my age group. Nothing too hectic there, a quiet lifestyle. No lager filled nightclub seeking gangs, in fact an area where one felt that little bit safer than downtown containing the hotspots which attracted youngsters and the not so young, who did not know when to stop.

Monica, like all women, likes to shop. She also likes to walk into a store and not shop at all after spending time trying on bracelets, necklaces, shoes etc. etc. etc. During these expeditions, I always carry a newspaper to stave off boredom. I am not a shopper.

One could see from outside the store that it was a real upmarket affair. The stuff in the window was priced to suit millionaires, not the likes of me.

Of course that particular type of establishment was just the kind of place to attract Monica, so in we went.

It was a narrow single storied store with long jewellery filled glass cases fronting passageways for the staff to move through. The walls behind were also covered with cases containing glittering, sparkling items of gold, diamonds and other expensive items.

One of the staff was at Monica's disposal in seconds and she was soon engaged in trying on and then rejecting various items of jewellery. I stood back and read my paper.

A man approached me from the far end of the store with that look of confidence which distinguished him from the rest of the staff. He was also dressed in a dark suit with matching tie, and gleaming white shirt.

I looked up and noticed a security camera just feet from me. That was it! I guessed he thought I was casing the joint or that I was maybe ready to smash and grab right now. I folded my paper and gave him what I thought was a smile of innocence.

Introducing himself as the manager, he inquired if he could help me. My response was in the negative, adding that I was only a poor hanger-on and certainly could not afford to buy anything in the store.

He laughed at this and I readily joined in, laughter being quite infectious. He told me that the store was one of part of a chain of seven and that he had been manager for two years. He was an extraordinarily effusive and friendly man and I was glad to have met him and have had such a nice time talking to him.

He then took me completely by surprise by asking if I would like a drink. It being a very hot day, I, of course, readily accepted and off he went to his office, soon to return with a silver tray containing two tall bottles of beer and chilled glasses.

I called to Monica and two chairs were produced, allowing us to sit at a glass topped display unit and imbibe

The manager was gone for some seconds, allowing me time to boast to Monica about my personality and chat getting us free beer when the manager returned, looked at me, started to say something, then hesitated and started again. *"Excuse me, excuse me Sir, but could I please look at your watch, if you would not mind, Sir."*

So that was it: he thought that my three year old fake Turkish bought Rolex was the real thing and that I was a richie in disguise!

Thinking very fast on my feet (which is quite unusual for me) I responded lordly *"This watch never leaves my wrist, my good man, I am sorry but that's it."*

With that, we finished our drinks and exited the premises.

This story is one of a number where my fake Rolex had impressed people no end. It just proves that status is all important to some people but not to me - honest!

Open and Shut

Micky 'The Lodger' Malone was known as one cute hoor. It was said that he could live in your right ear and rent out the left one as flats. He was also a member of a prominent political party until one day, he was caught taking a bribe from a known crossdresser. That proved to be the fatal blow, putting an end to his hopes of leadership of the party and his hopes of one day becoming leader of his country and codding people all of the time.

After the aforementioned scandal, Micky found it very hard to survive financially. He was also kicked out of the party as a lesson to others not to be caught taking bribes.

Micky soon teamed up with an old school chum, a man known as Patrick 'Fingers' O'Flaherty, who also lived by his wits.

Together they came up with a scheme so daring in its audacity as to be unbelievable and surreal but highly original in its content.

Micky arrived at the airport having disembarked from an incoming flight and was stopped by custom officials, he being known to all as one who would not be entirely on the straight and narrow.

There was very little in the large suitcase, just a shirt, a couple of pairs of socks and other odds and ends.

The officials were not happy with this, suspecting a crime of sorts. But after forcing the large piece of luggage through the X-ray machine, they discovered nothing and had to let him proceed.

The next week to the day, it was the turn of 'Fingers' O'Flaherty to alight from a plane. He was also stopped by customs and his large suitcase also searched. The customs men were again disappointed with their find, a swissroll with about two slices cut off, a full apple pastry and a vest. Fingers was also let go.

A week later it was the turn of Micky The Lodger again. The suitcase was opened to reveal one condom, an umbrella and a half eaten biscuit. The journey through the X-ray machine showed nothing.

The following week, it was Fingers again, this time the case contained one tie, a cheap gold plated medallion and a hard boiled egg. The officials requisitioned the egg, which they later included as an extra filling in their lunch break sandwich.

Weeks followed weeks and it was always either Micky the Lodger or Fingers O'Flaherty who would make their way through customs. They would be duly stopped and searched and suitcases opened but it always proved to be a futile exercise, for nothing was ever found.

This situation went on for many years and proved to be a means of lucrative incomes for both Mercy and Patrick. In fact, it set them up for life financially.

Essentially, the authorities never had the imagination to discover the true nature of the twisted duo. They had been smuggling duty payable contraband for a very long time under the noses of the customs men. The customs men hadn't realised that there was big money to be made in smuggling suitcases.

Out-Tray

I suppose what happened to Paddy Murphy could happen to anybody but I personally was still a bit surprised to say the least. Of course, hindsight tends to simplify the whole thing and cloud any thoughts of reflective rationale.

Paddy, you see was born with his hand out and was never of a mind to withdraw it - ever.

As he grew up, he developed a career as a bum, taking handouts wherever and whenever he could, without any trace of shame or discrimination whatsoever.

Paddy developed and grew into a strapping young man, while succeeding in avoiding labour of any description. While people would often discuss his inability and distaste for work, they would have to confess admiration of his hand, for its cleanliness, lack of welts and clean nails.

He was a regular feature outside the church every Sunday with his hand out, palm up, then outside the local football pitch later on, then all around the town that night and the other days to follow.

I heard that it was on a Wednesday morning that it happened but then it could have been on a Tuesday or even on a Thursday, you know how details become blurred after the event.

Paddy always slept with his left hand outside the covers with his palm turned up as was his habitual wont, but on this particular morning he awakened to find a tray attached to the open palm.

Try as he might, he was unable to remove the offending object and was eventually resigned to the strange situation of having a serving tray attached to him as part of his person.

From that day on, Paddy Murphy experienced a severe drop in

takings for people only laughed when he held the tray out in front of him calling out *"Any change, any change."* For some reason that Paddy could not fathom, people found this to be very funny and laughed at lot.

At about this time, Justin Desmond's Cafe was suffering the loss of its lone waitress Julie (Tango) Ahern who after getting her diploma in ballroom dancing decided to strike out and hit the big smoke in pursuance of her dream as a dancer on television and other places.

Just then, Justin, by an astoundingly amazing stroke of luck (or maybe because he was Catholic) chanced to meet Paddy Murphy walking through the street with fixed tray in hand, and dared to ask about Paddy's strange situation, while explaining his own tragic predicament regarding the loss of his diplomad dancing waitress to showbusiness.

Paddy reluctantly accepted Justin's offer of a job, after Justin pressed him on the matter, explaining that Paddy would be a natural at the waitering business but warning him that there would never be any chance for promotion while he carried a permanent tray.

Paddy was to carry on waiting on tables at Justin Desmond's for many years to come, never again being able to avoid work.

The unavoidable increase in business at Justine's Cafe was in no small way attributable to Paddy Murphy's tray, attracting visitors from miles around who would willingly queue just to see the trayed one.

And life went on.

Politics Crime and Other Horrors

Achieving the Impossible

Quincy Carter was a very popular man who loved life. His tall lean tanned figure and dark good looks were complemented by a wonderful personality and ready winning smile, which everyone found most attractive. Women flocked to him in their droves, but Quincy played the field, trying hard to please all by sharing himself out in his generous way.

Peg Tobin's arrival to work in the office on the floor below him was not exactly an earth-shattering event. She was diligent, hardworking, anxious to please and her work was faultless, but human nature being what it is and perception being that all important factor, meant that she was left very much to her own devices. Unfortunately for Peg, her physical construction was found to be a little off-putting to others of the species. Her large head and square shaped, plain features and wide, short, block squat body was found to be more than a little off-putting to others.

Quincy did not normally lunch in the company canteen, much preferring to eat out in more salubrious surroundings in one of the nearby eateries, but on this day the rain was heavy and the wind was high, so he decided to bestow the gift of his presence on his peers.

As Quincy entered the canteen, heads were raised in both admiration and envy at his glowing good looks, confidence and casual but stylish attire. He chose to bestow the honour of his presence on two of his fellow workers at a near table. They were delighted to be allowed to bask in the light of his personality.

Peg lifted her head from her large plate of meat pie with extra chips, and was just in time to witness the bright lights reflecting like a halo from the well gelled, luxuriously coiffured hair atop the smiling countenance of Quincy Carter. She stopped, her pie-filled fork held in mid air, amazed that a person of such beauty could exist. Nobody noticed her mesmeric state as she sat at the table alone and in love.

The large bunches of flowers started to arrive daily. Quincy was not surprised, being the kind of person he was. He was never even curious as to the identity of his secret admirer. The accompanying card was always signed with hugs and kisses, but again, being Quincy, this was only par for the course. In any case he gave the flowers away to be shared among his legion of female admirers and they loved him all the more.

Quincy imagined that he was being followed when he left work for home, but it was just a feeling and he could never see anybody, even when he would U-turn sharply and briskly retrace his steps. There was nobody ever to be seen.

The ground floor apartment which Quincy occupied had been carefully chosen for its central location and the fact that it fronted a little private circular grass area surrounded by a high fence where flowers and plants climbed, some succeeding in reaching the top. On sunny days Quincy would sit there on a bath towel, soaking up the sun's rays, adding to his already tanned hide.

The first letter was received with benign humour. It comprised ten pages in praise of Quincy. He finished reading the unsigned letter and concluded that it was only stating the obvious, before throwing it into the bin. Then there would be two letters a day, sometimes three. It began to irk him slightly. The flower deliveries also continued.

Peg looked in the mirror and saw the dimpled attractive face looking back at her. She knew that she was a little bit overweight and not as tall or attractive as other women but she knew that she possessed something that no other would ever match, sincerity and loyalty. She looked forward to the time when she would publicly declare her love for her handsome Quincy and he would return it. If Peg had nothing else, she had resolve.

At this stage of the game Quincy was starting to get a bit cheesed off. His boss was now complaining about the daily delivery of flowers and the necessary disposal of same and the repetitive nature of the letters praising him were really starting to get up his handsome nose.

Peg decided that the time was nearing. She would soon make her move. He was surely softening by now and must be madly curious as to who would declare her love for him by sending all of those bunches of flowers and go to the trouble of penning the wonderful love letters.

On opening the door of his apartment, Quincy was surprised to find and sense the smell of cooking. Puzzled, he walked to the door of the kitchen, easing it open to reveal the short broad bricklike figure of the disgustingly ugly women he had seen on one of his rare visits to the company canteen. Letting the door close, he slowly edged away wondering just what the hell was going on.

He should ring the police! Dropping his briefcase he was about to walk to the phone when the kitchen door swung open and the little squat woman came through carrying a large tray, laden with two plates, steam rising from the centred leg of lamb and sideplates of mixed vegetables.

She looked at him and smiled *"Welcome home darling ... perfect timing, sit down. I'll carve, or would you like to?"* Quincy looked at her with disbelief and slowly asked, *"What are you doing here?"* She had by now rested the tray on the table and was starting to place the hot plates on each side. Then lifting the steaming leg of lamb and the vegetables she also placed them on the table. Turning to face him, she spoke softly, asking *"Did you like the flowers and the letters? I meant every word you know. Nobody could ever love you as much as I do."* He looked at her, she was totally insane to imagine that he could love her. He did not even know her and did not want to know her, let alone love her.

Quincy's voice was loud and shrill, *"Get out, get out now you silly woman, get out!"* She looked at him with a sympathetic and understanding smile and responded quietly, *"It's me, Peg, now please sit down, darling, and we can talk about this over dinner."* Quincy closed his eyes, shaking his head to try and wake up from this bizarre nightmare. On opening his eyes he found she was still there, ugly, sitting and waiting. He advanced and without thinking grabbed the carving knife, plunging it into her chest again and again until she slid from the chair onto the expensive Persian rug. Quincy looked at the bloodied knife in his hand and then to the fallen body, trembling at the enormity of what he had done.

It took hours of shovelling to dig the hole in his little back garden. Because of the shape of the garden and of the body, Quincy decided to bury Peg standing up in a circular grave. He then spread the surplus earth all around the perimeter fencing covering some of his flowers and plants. When he had finished, he surveyed his handiwork and was well pleased with the end result. Nobody would ever find out.

One week later, after questioning, Quincy confessed to the crime. The police broke into her little apartment after Peg was reported missing. They were to find photographs of him walking home after work and letters dedicated to their future life together.

Quincy Carter had done something nobody had ever achieved before. He had actually succeeded in getting a square Peg into a round hole.

(Sick isn't it!)

The Gourmet Club

The tightly bound wire was starting to pierce his wrists. Droplets of blood fell on his face and neck causing him to gag. He felt ill from the force-feeding of the olive oil drenched mash of herbs and spices which also contained large garlic bulbs and thinly sliced truffle.

Albert O'Sullivan had pulled all available strings to get the young tearaway Mortimer the job as a Junior Reporter on the 'Clonard Echo.' Far from being grateful to his father, young Mortimer tended to do as little as possible, turning up late and then soon joining some of the older reporters to partake of long boozy 'lunches.' It took all of his father's persuasive powers and much pleading with his friend, the Editor, Cormac McSweeney. Cormac promised him six months, no more. If Mortimer did not pull up his socks by then, he would have to go.

The funny thing was that without much prompting young Mortimer was starting to operate, he was starting to develop a nose for news. There was first the case of pilfering from the local hospital. Without too much apparent effort Mortimer was able to link the story to a gang operating, using cleaners and security people, to accumulate a selection of drugs and goods, later destined for the black market. Because of his snooping the racket was exposed and all involved received appropriate sentences. He was soon on the trail of a stolen car scam and concluded his story to a successful end within weeks. Mortimer still went and drank at lunchtime, only now his craft was being honed to such an extent that nothing passed him by, any overheard conversation from something as simple as a remark about the weather to another mishap by a politician was to his interest.

The years rolled on and Mortimer achieved a degree of respect from his peers and was to be the recipient of a number of deserved awards for his investigative reporting. He developed a gregarious personality which caused him to be invited to many receptions, parties and lunches. He attended whenever he could. There was always a story.

It was at the Retirement Party of his boss Cormac McSweeney that he first heard mention of 'The Gourmet Club.' Turning around he witnessed the local Bishop Thomas Sweeney; Barry Kenny, the owner of the local golf course and Bill Ryan, M.D. of Ryan Engineering in deep conversation. Barry Kenny was the nearest of the three. Approaching slowly with glass in hand, Mortimer joined the trio. They were then discussing the qualities of the departing Editor and regretting his loss. After waiting for a gap in the conversation Mortimer asked, *"what is the Gourmet Club?"*

The trio looked at him with bemusement. Barry Kenny responded, "What, are you talking about?" Mortimer shook his head showing uncertainty. *"You did not mention the Gourmet Club?"* Barry laughed and was joined by his two companions. The Bishop chuckled deeply and pointed at Mortimer's glass, *"maybe you had one too many for the road."* Mortimer laughed with them and after some small talk soon drifted off into the crowd. Looking back from beyond the throng he could see the angry faces of the Bishop and Billy Ryan berating the now white-faced Barry Kenny. Mortimer wondered about all of this. Just what was 'The Gourmet Club,' and why the secrecy? Mortimer intended to find out.

Barry Kenny's phone rang some days later with an invitation from Mortimer to join him for a drink and address the question of golf and the amazing surging popularity of that game. It would certainly be of help to Barry, his business and his profile. Barry agreed to meet with him the following evening.

The 'Tee Room Bar' of the hotel was busy enough but not too busy that they were not able to secure a table by the window. After a couple of drinks and enquiring after each others families, Mortimer produced a tape recorder from his jacket pocket and proceeded to ask Barry about his business, his involvement in golf and his thoughts for the future of the game. The interview lasted about half an hour. Mortimer thanked Barry, laughed and said, *"And in conclusion now please tell me, what is the Gourmet Club?"* Barry moved uneasily in his chair and looked at Mortimer, showing bafflement on his pallid features. *"I, I don't know what you mean."* Mortimer continued, *"Ah come on, I heard you mention it at the reception. You, the Bishop and Bill Ryan, and I also saw you getting a telling off from them both after I left you. Now, do you want to tell me? What is the Gourmet Club?"* Barry arose quickly from his chair, knocking over his drink in the process, spilling it on the table causing his glass to roll slowly from the table to drop to the floor smashing to pieces. Mortimer was left to muse, after observing the nervy antics of Barry Kenny on being asked the question again. Mortimer was determined to get to the bottom of it all.

One evening, observing the large black saloon car outside the residence of Bishop Thomas Sweeney, Mortimer decided to call for a chat. The Bishop looked him straight in the eye and asked, *"Are you mad man, the Gourmet Club? I never heard of it!"* Mortimer sipped from the steaming coffee mug and searched the Bishop's face concluding that he was almost certainly lying, and was more determined than ever to find out why. They shook hands on Mortimer's leave, civil but now wary of each other.

The noise of clanking hammered steel was audible through the office walls of Ryan Engineering where sat Bill Ryan and Mortimer O'Sullivan in conversation. Mortimer saw no surprise on Bill Ryan's face at his unannounced visit and suspected that his call was expected. Bill Ryan opened his arms Christ-like and expressed annoyance at Mortimer's questions. *"You asked me the same stupid question at the Retirement Party for Cormac McSweeney and I am telling you for the last time, I do not know what you are talking about, and I would ask you to give up on this imaginary Gourmet Club."* Mortimer thought that there was some menace behind the laboured smile on Bill Ryan's face as they bade farewell.

The note left on his desk written in block lettering was short and to the point. *"The answer to your questions will be revealed tonight. Stay by your phone."* Mortimer decided that he would do just that.

It was 9.30pm and Mortimer sat at the phone wondering if the note was a hoax, a bit of tomfoolery on someone's part. Sitting back on his swivel chair he watched the smoke from his cigarette drift upwards to meet the long hanging light and decided to call it a day, maybe go for a drink before heading for home. Just then, the phone rang. Mortimer swiftly lifted it from its cradle and was surprised to hear the voice of his Bishop, Thomas Sweeney. The Bishop's voice sounded soft and friendly in its invitation to join him for a drink. Mortimer thought swiftly, was this the call he was waiting for? Instinctively, he decided to go for it. *"Yes, yes, of course, say ten-ish? See you then."*

Mortimer crossed the dark street pulling his collar tight around his neck in an attempt to keep out the chilly night wind. His watch showed 9.40pm. He would easily make it by ten. He wondered what he would find out. Maybe this was not the call he had been expecting at all. Whether or which it could prove to be a nice convivial evening. The Bishop was known to be a connoisseur of good liqueur.

Mortimer's thoughts were disturbed by the honking of a car horn and the calling out of his name. The sliding car window opened to reveal the jolly, ruddy face of Arty Houlihan, his butcher, beckoning to him. Mortimer ran to the car and gladly accepted the offer of a lift.
Arty glanced at Mortimer, showing some surprise. *"You too?"* 'Yes, the *Bishop also rang me tonight, well it won't do any harm to have a few jars and conversation."*

They were greeted at the large front door by the Bishop and ushered along the high ceilinged hallway to enter the sitting room which contained a large mahogany table where sat Barry Kenny; Bill Ryan; the well known Surgeon, Edmund Hickey; the retired Editor, Cormac McSweeney; a local politician by the name of Dermot O'Rourke, who true to form, quickly vacated his chair, offering Mortimer a strong well practised handshake, and Jonathan Williams, Mortimer's Bank Manager.

Bishop McSweeney stood at the head of the table and gently tapped his knuckles on its shiny surface in a call to order.

"*Gentlemen, we are gathered here tonight in an attempt to respond and satisfy Mortimer O'Sullivan's quest regarding his admirable endeavours in his queries and investigations regarding The Gourmet Club. The doors are secured, ensuring complete privacy so feel free to speak openly, but please fill your glasses first.*"

A large crystal goblet was placed in front of Mortimer and was quickly filled by the host, from the freshly uncorked bottle of rich light-reflecting port. The Bishop placed the bottle on the table at Mortimer's elbow.

Surgeon Hickey was the first to speak. In well modulated tones he suggested that it would be most civilised to first drink a toast to their visitor. All the company arose from their chairs and chanted, "*To Mortimer,*" then drinking from their glasses. As they resumed their seats Mortimer stood up, undecided as to what he would say, but settled for a short speech of thanks and then asked, "*Is this the Gourmet Club?*" The Bishop interjected, "*Yes, yes my son, but please, first have some more port and relax. Soon all your questions will be answered, deal?*" Mortimer smiled and nodded his head in agreement.

They were getting noisier and louder and their voices and laughter seemed to penetrate his brain. Mortimer slowly massaged both of his temples with his fingers hoping to get rid of the terrible pain. The figures sitting at the now floating table seemed to be featureless. Mortimer tried hard to focus, but failed. "*It was the port. The bastards must have put something in the port.*" Mortimer slipped into unconsciousness and his head fell forward, striking the table with a thud. He felt himself being lifted, carried out of the room and felt the crack as his skull hit the ceiling as he was being delivered down, down to a stinking place deep in the bowels of the earth.

On opening his eyes Mortimer observed his surroundings. Above him was a single hanging dim light bulb, swinging slowly, causing the shadows to move. His head still felt sore as if from a terrible hangover. On attempting to raise himself he realised that he was unable to. Raising his head to look down he found that his arms, torso and legs were bound tightly onto what appeared to be a hospital trolley. He also realised that every item of clothing had been taken from his body.

The pair entered the room chatting. Surgeon Hickey and the Butcher, Arty Houlihan. Surgeon Hickey approached first, smiled and said slowly and softly, *"Aah, I see that our intrepid reporter is awake."* Arty approached from behind Hickey and without saying anything started to touch and press Mortimer from his ankles up to his neck. *"Should be good, should be good."* They both walked behind him and proceeded to talk in whispers. There was the occasional laugh.

Mortimer shivered from fear and cold. He tried to scream but couldn't. Every fibre of his body screamed instead. What in the name of Jesus was going on? What were they doing to him, and why?

He felt the pain of the hypodermic needle being plunged into his arm, then saw the smiling face of Surgeon Hickey at his side. Before he drifted off, he heard the voice of the Butcher Arty Houlihan saying something about the problem with the length of a full leg and the necessary need to break it. His attempts to fight off the overpowering desire to sleep failed him.

Feelings of a tingling pain in his right leg caused Mortimer to wake up, slowly opening his eyes he was able to focus. Licking his lips he felt traces of olive oil and garlic around his mouth. He was no longer on the trolley, his only supports were the long length of wire stretching from a rusty steel ring on the ceiling down to his wrists, and a wide canvas band with a similar ceiling attachment which came down from his waist holding him solidly. But at least his area of vision was increased giving him a chance to look around at his place of imprisonment.

The walls to his left were of faded whitewashed stone, dripping with dampness. Stretching his head back behind him he was able to see what looked like a heavy wooden table, such as one might see in a butcher's shop. The tabletop glistened with what he imagined to be moisture. Turning his head towards the side of the room which contained the door he was then to witness something near the door also hanging from the ceiling. Closing his eyes and opening them again in order to improve his vision, he was able to see clearly. A leg, his leg, hung there, slowly dripping blood. If Mortimer's screams could be heard, nobody attended.

Now Mortimer knew. Now Mortimer understood exactly what 'The Gourmet Club' was.

Before he passed out, Mortimer could hear the far off sounds of fun, gaiety and the clinking of glasses.

Seán Taylor sat at what used to be Mortimer O'Sullivan's desk. Seán was young, bright and had that determination to succeed. He wondered about his missing predecessor and what had happened to him. He intended to make his mark. He was determined to find out. The first person he would speak to would be a man called Arty Houlihan. Arty was the last person to be seen speaking to the missing journalist as he drove him home on that fateful night. Lifting the phone directory Seán thumbed through the business section and eventually found the name under the heading 'Butcher.'
"Mr. Houlihan, can we meet. I'd like to ask you a few questions?"

Mirror Image

Mirrors are funny things, aren't they? When we look at our reflection do we really see ourselves as others see us or does our image show us someone completely different, I mean does anyone ever look in a mirror and think, "This is one ugly bastard." No, I don't think so!

The strangest case I ever heard in relation to mirrors concerned Gilbert Dawson who was known to be of average looks, worked as a librarian and was noted for his neat, fastidious nature and tidy mind. Gilbert could be seen extracting a comb or brush from his coat pocket on passing a shop window or on entering any premises containing a mirror and combing or brushing his mop of thick wavy hair. Mind you, his luxurious head did deserve such attention for it was the talk and envy of many a man not granted such hirsute blessings, as well as clear skin!

The first occurrence happened early one morning while Gilbert was shaving. He noticed a mark on his right temple. Turning his face nearer to the mirror to get a better view he was surprised to observe what could only be described as a wart close to his right ear. Gilbert was very perplexed by this. Warts don't grow overnight, do they? On his arrival at the library that same morning Gilbert immediately went to the staff bathroom to have another look at the intrusive growth but to his surprise his reflection showed only flawless skin. After examining his countenance from ear to ear he could only conclude that the morning wart experience must have been a figment of his imagination, but nevertheless Gilbert visited the bathroom more than usual that day just to be on the safe side but was not to find any kind of blemish whatsoever.

The next morning proved to be sunny and bright, providing Gilbert Dawson with a sense of feelgood and happiness, that is until he entered the bathroom and looked in the mirror. The wart was back, only this time it was accompanied by a pockmarked zone right in the centre of his chin. The wart itself had grown larger. The eyes in the mirror stared back at Gilbert showing bewilderment and incomprehension. He shaved and washed before applying ointment on the unwanted pockmarks on his chin and set off for work.

At the office, having raced to the bathroom, Gilbert felt his chin in bewilderment. The reflected face showed only a clear, cleancut face with nary a sign of the early morning marks. He spent a full fifteen minutes in his staff bathroom examining every part of his face for blemishes, but to no avail. His face was completely clear.

The next morning Gilbert entered his bathroom with not a little trepidation. On facing the mirror he was confronted with the sight of a face now covered with warts and so pockmarked as to be quite frightening. Also his hair had receded to such an extent that he looked like a circus clown, a dangerous circus clown. Gilbert rang for the doctor to call before contacting his place of work pleading illness.

The doctor was mystified, *"But your face is clear, no marks whatsoever and your hair is not falling out."* The doctor prescribed some relaxants, muttering *"nutcase"* to himself on leaving.

Now it was the nose! What had once been an honest to God, straightforward, normal nose was now crooked and bent. There were also two of his upper front teeth missing. Gilbert leaned on the sink looking directly into the mirror, gazing at himself. The eyes which stared back at him looked hostile and unfriendly. Attempting a smile reflected only a gap-toothed grimace.

Gilbert Dawson felt that he was losing his mind. Wouldn't you?

Gilbert spent the next day and the day after in bed, afraid to look at the mirror again. On the third day he plucked up his courage and decided to face the music and the mirror. Walking into the bathroom he slowly edged his frame along the wall holding the mirror. The reflection which faced him turned his blood cold.It showed him a wart-covered face with deep pockmarked patches covering both his countenance and hairless head, only this time the face in the mirror was smiling - a grotesque smile of satisfaction. Gilbert gripped the sink in fear and despair. He decided to get to the phone and ring for his doctor again, but before he could, the two hands of his reflection came out through the mirror catching him by the neck and hauling him roughly through to the other side.

He woke up to find himself sitting in a tiny dark space, the only light coming from a mirror on the wall. Raising himself to look at the mirror, he was just in time to see the reflection of his old self lift a hammer and smash the mirror to pieces. Gilbert was left in total suffocating darkness.

True Love

The hot sun beat down relentlessly on the smouldering rocks scattered about the vast desert area. The air hung motionless and still. A sidewinder twisted its way from the shelter of one boulder to another in its hunt for survival.

"Irene, goodnight Irene, I'll see you in my dreams." The sound of Willie Nelson's voice broke the silence and burst forth from the open windows of the saloon car as it sped along the dust covered road leaving a cloud of fine dust to rise momentarily, soon to settle and rest, succeeding in covering any signs of intrusion.

Wilbur held the steering wheel lightly while singing along with one of his favourites, Willie Nelson. As he always told Clara, Willie Nelson was the greatest. He did not just sing songs of love, he sang songs of love with love. Wilbur sang the last line turning up the volume on the radio as he did, *"I'll see you in my dreams."*

Wilbur also sang himself, being the possessor of a fine voice he was a long-time member of the church choir and was always invited to sing at social gatherings, parties and weddings.

Taking one hand from the wheel Wilbur gently nudged Clara asking, *"Well, well, what did you think of that?"* Wilbur expected a little bit of praise on his singing but he got only silence. She probably was still cross after the last argument. They were quarrelling a lot lately. Wilbur had found out about the affair only by chance.

His insurance business was healthy but the nature of the work dictated that he spend long hours away from his beloved Clara. So Clara met Carlos Dureldo, a young waiter and engaged in an affair with him. Clara was not discreet and the scandal was soon the talk of the community, inevitably reaching the ear of Wilbur through the good offices of a member of the choir. Wilbur was shocked but took enough time to take stock of the situation and map out a plan of action to win back the affection of his beloved Clara.

Glancing towards her Wilbur admired Clara's long blonde hair, as the breeze swept it back from her pretty head, only adding to her beauty. Wilbur had turned off the radio some good fifteen minutes ago hoping for some sort of communication but there was nothing, his attempts at conversation were in vain. Clara just sat there looking straight ahead, pale faced and silent. She would eventually come around. Wilbur was convinced of that.

The confrontation with Clara did not go as Wilbur had expected. When he first broached the subject Clara readily admitted to the affair, showing both defiance and anger, telling Wilbur that they had married far too young and that they now should consider divorce.

While Clara talked, Wilbur thought what they needed was a break, a holiday, a change. Wilbur could not comprehend the Clara who had stood before him spitting out words of hatred and resentment. Letting her ramble on, Wilbur decided on a vacation.

Clara eventually sat on the passenger seat of the car next to Wilbur, but only after a lot of effort and stress on his part. Once her initial reluctance was overcome, Clara went quite and acquiescent, seeming to accept the changed situation.

Looking ahead, Wilbur watched the magical water-like mirage reflecting on the shimmering tarmac and said a silent prayer of thanks to God. Clara, the love of his life sat at his side, the sun was shining and they were on vacation together. Things would soon be patched up. Clara was not talking to him but that was something Wilbur accepted completely, understanding the circumstances. Wilbur was happy to see the sign saying 'Fuel, provisions ahead,' saying to Clara, *"One small stop sweetheart, from here on we go forward with a full tank towards a new dawn."* Reaching over he gave her arm a gentle squeeze.

After telling the lone, aged attendant to, *"Fill her up,"* Wilbur asked Clara if she needed to use the ladies room. There was no response. Wilbur did not despair, he would win her back again, just as he had won her love all those years ago. Wilbur went from the car and paid the attendant, then sat back again behind the wheel and drove off in a flurry of dust. The old attendant made his way back to the worn shack, away from the pumps, but before he could make it to the phone, his stomach erupted causing him to spew gastric bile on the side of the hut, fear and disgust showing in his wide-eyed features.

Wilbur was stopped at a police roadblock soon after. He was ordered out of the car, told to walk towards the police car with his hands in the air and was arrested handcuffed and ensconced in the caged rear seat.

The swarms of flies busily feeding off the rotten stinking corpse sitting in the passenger seat were not to be put off by the police who reluctantly approached the scene, armed only with their ignorance of Wilbur's insanity.

Timeshare

Philip's instructions were made crystal clear. During the many training sessions he had been told repeatedly to ingratiate himself with the punter. Find out what they worked at, what their hobbies were and relate to them regarding their likes and dislikes. Tell them a story of his own upbringing, manufacture a sad and unhappy background if necessary. Essentially it as all about getting them to part with a large deposit while promising them holidays in exotic places of beauty at a reduced cost which would never be repeated. Most important of all the word 'Timeshare' was never to be used, the term was now 'Part Ownership.' Philip did not have to be told to be charming, that was a natural asset he possessed.

Sunny Lanzarote's little streets were teaming with tourists, hawkers, menu displaying waiters, Africans waving shining cheap watches, ice-cream vendors, the wonderful smells of grilled fish wafting inviting along the walkways and youngsters of different nationalities spaced well apart in groups of two's offering scratch cards and the chance to win a free immediate prize. To collect a reward one only had to attend at the Hotel De Luxe. Taxi's would be called for and the unsuspecting prospects would be delivered to meet the masters of the hard sell.

The man was tall, angular and somewhat gawky looking, wearing tan coloured open sandals which matched his stylish shorts and top. Expensive looking dark sunglasses enhanced his leathered well tanned skin. The baseball cap was pulled down on his forehead making it difficult to discern his features. As he was ushered to the taxi with scratch card in hand he wondered about all of this. But the taxi was free and he kept an open mind. Maybe there was no catch, maybe there was a free prize. He was a man of means and did not really need to take this journey to collect some little gift but he thought that it might turn out to be an adventure, something to do for an afternoon, a little diversion. He sang softly to himself, singing in a language the driver failed to understand.

Philip sat at one of the many neatly laid out tables and mused as he waited for the next prospect. He thought about his past life and his ambition to succeed in this business. His given target was one sale per week. He always achieved this and more, giving him a decent bonus.

It was not that life was tough in London, nor even the miserable weather that had driven him to seek sanctuary in this sunny place. It was the break-up of his marriage of ten years which he could not take. He left her the house, he left her with everything and struck out to find another life in another place. After working in Timeshare for over three years now, he was starting to find himself. He was starting to live again. He would return every night to the little house in the mountains where he would be greeted by his loving partner Maria with an enveloping embrace.

Philip was shaken from his thoughts by the arrival of his supervisor, a hard faced male by the name of Tom Robinson who was leading a tall man wearing tan coloured shorts and a baseball cap. Tom Robinson invited the man to sit at the table facing Philip and departed.

Reaching across the table Philip shook the man's hand while introducing himself. The questionnaire in front of him had to be filled out first. It still surprised Philip that people were so willing to give personal information to total strangers. "Suckers," he thought.

Before asking any questions Philip went through the usual ritual of asking the man if he was enjoying his holiday and other such small talk. Producing a pen from his jacket top pocket Philip proceeded to question him. This would establish the man's financial status. The man gave his name as Andrei Chereshnev. Date of birth - 22nd May 1944. Place of birth - Moscow. Occupation - Researcher. Income - the man smiled and said softly, *"More than you will earn in a lifetime."*

Philip knew that his case was lost unless he could discover Andrei's income. He could not afford to hazard guessing, but experience had taught him that there were many paths to take, any one of them eventually leading him to discover the man's worth. If his income was below a certain figure Philip would terminate the meeting on some pretext and would be passed on to another visitor. Philip had developed and cultivated guile in a most professional way.

Andrei Chereshnev's answer left Philip in some puzzlement. *"People, you research people? How, how is that done?"* Andrei forced a smile and responded. *"It is very exclusive, it is very unique, it is very individual."* This one was going to be tough. This was going to be a challenge but Philip always rose to a challenge.

Andrei accepted Philip's offer of a drink and they adjourned to the empty sprawling bar laid out with cushioned wicker chairs surrounding large glass topped tables. Philip's past experience told him that the prospect would normally soften and mellow after a few drinks, eventually giving enough information for him to form an opinion in calculating the prospective buyers income.

Philip sipped from his tankard of beer and watched as Andrei drank from a tall vodka filled glass. He accepted the offer of a second drink and then a third. The baseball cap and sunglasses still covered his greying head and eyes. Philip found this to be a little disconcerting, not to be able to see the Russian's eyes. He had learned that the eyes could be read, giving him an insight into the mind and intentions of a prospect. Andrei was now more inclined to talk and listened, show-ing some dismay on hearing of Philip's plight regarding the break-up of his marriage and the eventual climb back to sanity. Philip even managed to draw tears to his eyes in relating his sad past, accepting the offer of a handkerchief from Andrei to dab away the tears.

Looking through his tear filled eyes Philip was delighted to notice that the man's lips were pursed and grim, his head slowly shaking from side to side in sympathy. It was in the bag.

Philip apologised for his breakdown and after dabbing his eyes for the last time he produced the questionnaire from an inside pocket and laid it on the table. Sniffing, he asked Andrei if he was willing to reveal his income.

Andrei Chereshnev hesitated a little, smiled and said, *"I charge fifty thousand American dollars for every subject. I am self employed and I never take more than four commissions a year. Now you know my income, but my profession is one availed of by International Government Agencies and some Multinational Corporations My work is of a vocational nature and the ethics of the work dictate complete secrecy on my part."*

All Philip now needed was Andrei's Credit Card Number and so allow the company to withdraw the large amount adding to Philip's own income.

But Philip was curious and decided to play the Russian along and try to wheedle some more information from him. Philip knew that the sale was now safe. Returning from the bar with a bottle of vodka, a jug of ice and a tankard of beer he sat opposite Andrei and spoke to him in tones of friendship and camaraderie. The tall Russian took the generosity as it was given. He was now very relaxed and easy. Philip decided the time was ripe to pursue his interest in Andrei'a occupation. The bottle was depleted and the glass lay empty on the slightly moist table.

Smiling a winning smile Philip asked Andrei, *"It would make it a lot easier for me to have the questionnaire filled in its entirety. Can I ask you again what your occupation is, please?"* Andrei said nothing for a while then speaking slowly and softly said, *"Nobody knows what I do, it is better that you do not know."* Philip persisted using all his charm and deceit. Andrei eventually agreed, telling Philip, *"You will never tell anybody else."* Philip agreed.

At Andrei's request they moved to a quiet spot at the far end of the gardens at the rear of the hotel to be away from the ears of others.

Philip was intrigued by the secrecy of it all and was quite excited in anticipation and curiosity. He stood and watched as the tall Russian walked amongst the bushs surrounding them, checking that nobody was within earshot. Seeming satisfied Andrei returned to stand close to his new found friend.

"Well? ... Well?" asked Philip, anxious to find out.

Andrei reached down to open a zip in a pocket of his shorts and produced a sheath which exposed a dagger handle. Taking the blade from its casing he smiled, lovingly touching the sharp serrated edge with his fingers.

"This my friend, is one of my most trusted aids. It is silent and effective, easy to carry and is easy to hide on one's person. It took a lot of time and effort on the part of your wife to contact me. I was actually thinking of retiring but when she told me of your cruelty and the many beatings she suffered at your hand I simply could not refuse her request. That and half of the large insurance pay-out she will receive on your death."

Philip tried to make his escape but was quickly and expertly hugged close to his adversary and felt the sharp knife hitting his chest. The first blow caused blood to spurt from the spewing cavity causing Andrei to dance to one side to avoid the shower. The knife was stuck in again and again until the lifeless Philip was let loose and allowed to drop slowly to the ground.

Andrei walked the short distance to the beach while tearing up the questionnaire into tiny pieces and then after rubbing the weapon and his hands in the sand he removed his sandals and walked to the water allowing the waves to wash away the blood and sand. Nobody took any notice of the tall man as he jumped in the water laughing at his own silliness in failing to avoid some of the faster flowing high waves.

The following days newspapers reported on the murder of a Timeshare Representative found in a secluded area in the grounds of the Hotel De Luxe in Lanzarote. His estranged wife who lived in London was too distraught to comment.

The Cycle

Her dark eyes shimmered and glittered, reflecting the wayward flickering of the candle at the centre of the small table separating us in the dimly lit bar. Her voice was pleading as she repeated it again. *"I am here to warn you, you are to be terminated, please believe me."*

I knew exactly what she meant and that she meant what she said. While I absorbed the message I studied her and could not but admire the young thing. Her eyes were brown, with skin the colour of bronze highlighted by a mass of curling jet black hair. The soft accented voice was repeating the mantra again. But how did she know? How did she know of me and my activities? I intended to find out, but not now, not here. I would get her someplace quieter, someplace where there would be no witnesses. After all, I was a professional and there was never an occasion where I ever failed. They always talked. If you were tied up and made to watch as your fingers were cut off one by one, wouldn't you?

In my long career as a member of the agency, I had always been very diligent, ever careful to cover my tracks. As the years rolled by and my hair turned to grey, it became even easier to kill and escape. After all, who would ever suspect an ageing old duffer like me of being an assassin?

On my last two assignments I actually rang for the police and then waited outside the respective buildings of the targets, where I watched as they rushed past me in response to my call reporting mutilation and murder. On the second occasion, a policeman stopped to question me, asking if I had seen anyone leaving the building. My slowly spoken negative response seemed to annoy the man enormously, while giving me great satisfaction. Fools!

She refused my request as to how she knew me and my business but I was not too worried about that. She would talk - in time.

I married once but it did not last. I suppose my long absences were not conducive to any kind of a lasting relationship. In any case, my job came first. My very first assignment was a hit on a man in a wheelchair. Don't ask me who he was for I was never told his name, only that I was driven to a big house in the country and while the driver waited, I shot the cripple through the window and kept firing until the gun clicked empty. I took some seconds to admire my handiwork and was later able to note in my report that his brains ended up just between his shoulder and his chest. This seemed to impress my superiors a lot and I received a bonus with my next pay check. That same week my boss shook my hand telling me I was a natural and that I would go far.

She knew my name of course but she refused any details except to tell me that she was called Maria. She was now talking to me again, "*The way I see it you have two choices, you can go to ground and stay there severing all contact with the organisation, or you can stay and be killed, I pray that you make the right decision.*" Maria looked at me long and hard as if trying to read my mind but I think she knew that it was a foregone conclusion that I was not one to back off. Anyway, what else could I do - go to some fecking retirement home and mix with the blue rinse brigade. No way!

It was then that I felt that first slug enter me, hitting me in the lower part of my stomach, the noise muffled by the silencer attached to the gun Maria held under the table. She looked at me with a look of detachment on her face as she pulled the trigger a second time. I felt the jolt of pain as the projectile hit me and as I started to fade I could not help but admire her audacity and calmness as she did her work. She would go far.

Reunion

The other members of the board were put there just to give the illusion of democracy but really everyone was aware of their place and never crossed swords with their Chairman and Chief Executor Roland Bateman. After all, the company was Roland's baby, it was Roland's creation and he was not averse in pointing this out to anybody who might be inclined to disagree with any of his dictates.

It was not just Roland's strong personality which influenced the board members, it was his hard, tough and ruthless character which impressed them most. They crossed Roland at their peril.

Roland was a driven man. His ambition leading him along the road to more wealth, power and utter selfishness. He, in fact, displayed all of the characteristics of a tortured soul, and Roland, in fact, was tortured by his past.

Roland was aged three, his brother Denis, only one year younger when the tragedy occurred. They were subject to constant bickering and sometimes violent differences between their parents carried out without thought for the frightened children who could only cry in fear and non-comprehension.

On that fateful night they could only shiver and quake. With tear filled eyes they watched numb with fear as the man they called Daddy held their mother against the wall pummeling her with his strong clenched fists until she stopped resisting and slipped to the floor, her eyes staring and lifeless, blood pouring from her mouth.

The two children were found the next day huddled close to the corpse of their mother. Their father's car was found in the river, some two weeks later. His body sitting in the driver's seat, fists still tightly clutching the steering wheel.

The two boys were moved to an orphanage where the regime was cold and strict. Whilst theirs was a special case, it was still just that, a case. After six months Denis was fostered out to a couple. At first they would bring him to meet Roland for a few hours at weekends. The frequency of the visits decreased until eventually they ceased.

Over the years Roland was passed from one institution to another, all condemning his wild rebellious bullying ways and his total lack of respect for authority. Roland used his lonely nights to sob, his mind shaping into a warped vessel, filled with hatred for others. The image of his mother's murder was slowly easing from his mind but he could still feel the touch of his brother's hand in his, looking up at him, seeking comfort.

Others said Roland was lucky but Roland created his own luck. Life on the street taught him all about people and life. "Do unto others before they do it to you," was a practice which served him well. He rented a ramshackle shed buying and selling anything and everything, no questions asked. The business flourished, Roland soon moving to a larger premises which he also used as an office for his new import/export business. The small hardworked staff he employed were to learn of his fierce temper, realising that there was something very wrong with the mind of their employer.

Roland Bateman's empire was widespread, covering everything from construction to retail clothing to electronics. Investors were always assured of a decent return on their capital.

During his early business years Roland had made enquiries about his long last brother Denis, in an attempt to trace him. Apparently the foster parents whose names he had established as Ellen and Walter Peters had adopted Denis shortly before emigrating to America. Roland had employed a detective agency but the trail was old and cold and despite their best efforts the family were never traced.

Roland's house lay in a quiet select area separated from his neighbours by a high fence giving him the solitude he desired. The motorway was a mere two miles away. Once on the motorway, depending on traffic, he could be in his office in an hour and a half, give or take.

Lifting the phone from its cradle Roland heard the voice of his secretary telling him with some hesitancy that *"There was a person on the line with an American accent, claiming to be Roland's brother, would he take the call? Line six."*

"Roland?" the soft American voice asked. *"Is that really you?"* Emotions arose in Roland's being, emotions long buried and forgotten, preventing any immediate response. The voice asked, *"Roland? Roland?"* Roland gasped a trickling slow response, swallowing hard, attempting to smother the rising sentiment.

"Denis, oh Denis, I tried to find you, I tried ... I tried, tell me, please tell me, how did you find me?" Roland's voice now sounded like that of a child in innocent questioning sobs. The voice of his brother responded to him - also in slow tearful words. *"Your photograph on the cover of Newsweek last month, I just knew it was you, I knew it was my big brother."* Roland blew his nose in his handkerchief 'composure ... composure.'

On hearing that his brother was in town staying in a hotel and was driving a rented car Roland immediately ordered Denis to pack his bags, get a map and drive to Roland's house which from now on was to be regarded as a home from home for whatever length of time or forever.

Roland's secretary was mystified, *"All today's meetings off? No more phone calls?"*
The directions were made very clear to his brother. Roland had repeated them twice to be sure. He wondered if he looked like him, if there would be any similarities - were there any family traits? Roland left his offices in a state of anxious excitement. The engine of his car purred into life at his touch, seemingly joining him in his state of euphoria.

Ignoring any speed limits Roland put his foot down hard on the accelerator, driving in the fast lane, flashing his lights and thumping his horn at anyone unlucky enough to be in his speeding path. He soon approached the slip road which led him to the last two twisting miles to meet his long lost brother.

Roland tried on a number of occasions to pass out the little open-topped sports car ahead, but the lady driver with the long flowing breeze swept blonde hair seemed oblivious to the loud honking and flashing of Roland's car. It was at the dangerous bend at the top of a hill, just near the edge of the deep quarry that Roland's rage overtook him. Pressing his foot down hard on the accelerator he advanced at speed, hitting the sports car, causing it to lurch forward unable to take the corner. The car went straight through the wire fencing, striking a rock causing it to roll, turning over a number of times before bursting into flames as it finally landed at the bottom of the quarry.

Roland stopped his car to inspect it for damage. There was not a mark, not a sign of anything that could connect him to the crash. He drove off, this time with a clear road ahead, his anger subsided.

There was no sign of any other car in the spacious area fronting the house. Roland was glad. He would much prefer to be there ahead of his brother and give him a proper welcome.

The police car arrived some hours later to inform him of a serious accident down the road. A car had crashed through the fence at the bad bend, probably driving too fast and going out of control. The body of a woman was found near the burned out vehicle. *"There was a handbag containing the cover page of Newsweek magazine with a picture of Roland Bateman. There was also a diary containing notes by one Denise Peters, was he expecting her? How well did he know her?"*

The policemen were saddened by Roland's reaction. All he did was to howl and cry out in large bursts of sorrow, tears streaming down his cheeks. They figured it must have been someone very close to him.

Incisive Action

Vincent Butler held the head of the brush in both hands, thumping the attached handle into the floor vigorously. He succeeded in rejoining both parts together. His starting time was nine o'clock, but, Vincent diligently turned the key in the lock at eight thirty every morning and would give the little barber's shop an early brush up and dusting. After all, all of this would, one day, be his.

Vincent had served his time as a youth under Sylvie Cotter over thirty years ago and had proved to be a most loyal and responsible employee. Particularly at times such as Sylvie's heart attack, four years ago, when Vincent single handedly ran the business, some said nearly as well as Sylvie, if not better. Even when Sylvie returned to work, Vincent would insist that he take it easy and slow down. Vincent had decided many years before that loyalty would pay and that if he gave Sylvie his all, he would eventually end up in Sylvie's position. His business plan was very simple. All that was needed was to knock down the timber wall covering the space under the stairs making room for another sink and four chairs and with an apprentice to help, Vincent could increase turnover by about fifty per cent. That was his dream.

Sylvie Cotter felt unwell and realised that he would soon have to give in and take heed of his doctor's orders. It was expected that he would leave the business to Vincent Butler and that expectation was entirely correct, for no man had ever given the time, respect and honour that Vincent gave to his boss Sylvie.

Oliver Tweed listened on the phone, nodding his head now and again in comprehension. "Yes, the business transfer documentation is quite straightforward. Your requirement is simply to transfer the business from your name to Vincent Butler. Is that correct Mr. Cotter? Yes, yes, you can call in to sign some time after my holidays. I'll be gone for two weeks. No problem, goodbye Sir." Oliver returned the phone to its resting place and speculated about the generosity of his client Sylvie Cotter and what a really nice man he was.

Vincent was surprised at the arrival of the handyman Percy Cadogan, paints and brushes in hand, informing Vincent that his instructions were to paint the walls and ceiling, install a new sink, change the mirrors and lay down a roll of linoleum, adding something about a change of ownership, querying Vincent about the possibility of the sale of the business. Vincent's response was negative and muted, the fear which gripped his heart prevented him from any logical thought.

Sylvie had decided to do it in style. If he was going to leave the business to his faithful employee, at least he would leave it in good nick and had already written a short speech of thanks to Vincent for his years of loyalty. He looked forward to the day of the surprise presentation of the deeds and the key to the front door.

Sylvie Cotter decided not to attend at his little barber's shop for a while if only to give Vincent and Percy Cadogan some space. The hours progressed into days and there was still no sign of Sylvie. Vincent was beside himself with hurt, fear and rage as the days went by. He decided that at the very first opportunity he would tackle Sylvie head on. In any case he now had nothing to lose.

Vincent waited, white coated with his three combs displayed on the top pocket and watched as Percy cleaned his brushes preparing to take his leave. It was now well over two weeks since he had last heard from his boss and the omens looked bad. He once again promised Percy to inquire from his boss if he would consider selling the shop to Percy's son-in-law, who badly needed more office space for his successful haulage business.

It was another two days before Sylvie decided to show his face. He arrived at the shop with a somewhat smug self-satisfied look. Before changing into his work coat he produced a long bulky envelope from the inside pocket of his jacket, placing it carefully on a shelf between them. Catching Vincent's eye in the large centre mirror Sylvie winked and gave a smile of satisfaction. Vincent turned his head away, unable to respond. That morning the little shop was quite busy, each of the two barbers handled at least a dozen customers. What struck Vincent more than anything else was the casual and relaxed manner of Sylvie.

He also looked better than he had for years.

Just before lunch time Sylvie was down to his last client when the man decided to tell him a joke, something about an elephant and a flea. Sylvie listened and then laughed loudly, at the same time catching Vincent's scowling face in the mirror.

Vincent could take no more. Grabbing a scissors he ran at Sylvie in a frenzy and plunged it into him, again and again, stopping only when his arm wearied of the thrusting actin. The blood splattered client just sat there on the chair, white-faced and shocked.

Nobody could ever figure out why on the very day that his boss was going to hand over the business, Vincent decided to murder him. There were some jokes of very bad taste circulating about bad haircuts and such like but Vincent did not much appreciate such jokes as he sat in his cell and contemplated the vagaries and quirks of life and death.

Stiletto Joe

Oliver C. Johnstone's second book was as popular as its forerunner, also achieving the added financial bonus of being translated into forty or so different languages. His literary efforts were at last being recognised. Two bestsellers in two years was something of a rare feat in that business.

After years of rejection by all the bigger publishers, Oliver eventually found Henry Wright, who, after years of publishing blue chip projects like 'Greenfingers Guide,' and some travel books, took a chance on Oliver by publishing his fast paced murder novel. A thriller, its central character being a sadistic killer by the name of 'Stiletto' Joe Crane who murdered at will.

The difference in Oliver's works and most other books written in that genre was that the villain of the piece Joe Crane, was not just a killer, he was an extremely clever man who used a stiletto as his weapon. This was a means of identification, identifying him as being different to all other common or garden assassins. After each murder he would send handwritten notes to the media and to the police, detailing the torturous murders, teasing and goading the police and mocking them on their inability to find him. Oliver's creation was intellectually superior and the first book's enormous success naturally spawned the second, turning both Oliver and Henry Wright into wealthy men. The reading public clamoured for more. The other major difference was that at the end of each story, the psychopathic Joe Crane was left to get away scot-free.

Oliver's insight into the terrible mind of Joe Crane was starting to affect him insofar as that Oliver himself abhorred violence and also the way some tabloid reports of lunatic copycat killings decided him on a course of action that would change the fate of Stiletto Joe in his current and last novel. He would kill him off at the end, making sure that he would die as grisly a death as he had delivered to others.

Stiletto Joe was getting careless in his arrogance. His latest victims was still alive despite mutilation and torture at the hands of Crane. Joe left the bedroom, slowly washing his blood covered hands, singing softly to himself then methodically wiping the sink clean of fingerprints, taking the soft towel to his forehead to dry off the tiny specks of blood. Hearing screams, he turned and ran to the doorway of the small apartment.

His victim had somehow managed to crawl to the door and was now lying between the open door and the frame, the room trailed with his blood. The shrieks of the two old ladies were loud and continuous, drawing more people from surrounding apartments.

Joe rushed out through the door, pushing the two women to one side and ran for the stairway trying to cover his face with one hand. But at least a dozen people were later able to give the police a description. They each in turn told of seeing a tall man, balding, dressed in a dark suit, running along the hallway, some had also seen what looked like a strawberry birthmark behind his right ear.

Oliver's appearance on the highly rated 'Patrick Howard Show' was at his own request. Dismissing any notions that he was capable of any wrong-doings by any nutters out there, he disclosed that he was in the process of killing off his murderous creation. He wouldn't tell too much so as not spoil it for his readers but he was on his last chapter of the trilogy and would make sure that Joe Crane would get his just desserts. Joe would end up a lot worse than any of his victims. This should satisfy his detractors.

The large penthouse apartment Oliver now inhabited suited him admirably, as indeed did his single status. His address was known only to some family members and to his publisher. The solitude was totally conducive to his work. He already had an idea for his next novel. It would not matter too much whatever his subject might be for Oliver was now an established writer and anything he wrote would sell.

As Oliver C. Johnstone was about to sit at his computer and start the beginning of the end of Joe Crane, he heard a gentle tapping on his door. He looked at his watch. It was a little after eight, dusk was falling. Whoever it was would get very short shrift from Oliver. There was work to be done and a murder to complete.

The tall, balding man dressed in black pushed Oliver back into the room quickly closing the door with his foot, keeping Oliver in his vision. Holding the very frightened writer in a tight hold with his left hand around Oliver's neck, he produced a long stiletto knife plunging it into his victim's neck, then pulling it out to pepper Oliver's body with slow measured blows.

Before Oliver slid to the floor in death, he managed to see an ugly red mark behind his attacker's right ear and the last words he heard were whispered quietly in his ear - *"Nobody kills me off."*

Flower Power

Craig Brandon was popular, gregarious, possessing a fluency of speech and a sense of fun which endeared him to all. His sporting achievements were still remembered and the combination of his friendly personality and witty comments on life in general made him a much admired figure. His occasional television appearances as a sporting commentator only added to the generously granted status as something of a folk hero. Craig relished the attention he got, but behind the facade of projected humour and the acceptance as a character of personality, lay an increasingly bitter man, full of resentment and envy.

June was kind and loving - if only she had someone to love her. Her lonely life was some bit assuaged by her interest in her exotic plants and flowers. June suffered the loneliness of a married widow. Despite Craig's resentment and long time lack of interest in her she forgave him, understanding his needs and wants, which did not include her. Ten years of marriage had honed her understanding of him.

The glass covered front porch contained her large collection of plants and flowers which she lovingly tended daily. She talked to her plants and they in turn blossomed and bloomed, giving her some degree of happiness.

In the early days June had visited a number of different doctors, but the prognosis was always the same. There was nothing wrong with her. She was quite capable of having a child. She never told Craig and took the blame herself.

June knew that Craig despised her, but she still could not tell him the truth. It would hurt him too much.

'The Barren Bitch' was one of Craig's favourite descriptions of her. He resented her with a vengeance. He had no reason to rush home, June's acquiescent simpering manner annoyed him. She actually spoke to those fecking plants and flowers. He had long stopped having sex with her. To Craig, the marriage had become a habit, no family, just her and her stupid plants. He punished her with occasional drunken beatings. She did not ever complain and Craig despised her all the more.

Craig had met Lynn some months previously in his local pub which was festooned with photographs of his past sporting glories. Lynn was duly impressed. Lynn proved to be the most attentive lover he had ever encountered and they would meet regularly at her apartment. She worked as a senior executive with a major brokerage company, where she had bedded many of the senior directors to achieve her present status. When she became pregnant by the vice-president of the company, a happily married man, there was one easy course of action she could take. Lynn rang Craig and arranged a meeting. They met in a quiet corner of the bar. When Craig was told the news he was overjoyed.

June, of course, refused his request for a divorce despite many threats and tantrums. She cried and pleaded with him to stay with her, she loved him. She had nothing but him and her plants.

But Craig wanted to marry the woman he loved, he wanted to marry the mother of his child, so he decided that if his wife would not divorce him, he would have to consider other alternatives.

He surprised June one evening by arriving home early while she was tending her plants. For the first time in years he was kind to her, producing a bottle of wine for them to share. June had been longing and hoping for change and reconciliation, she had always known in her heart that this moment would come, because deep down she knew Craig was a good man. She lifted her glass to toast.

He watched her as she drank, the drug slowly taking affect, then her body jerking spasmodically in pain. Looking at her eyes, all Craig saw was a look of understanding and sadness, more than anything else. All June saw in Craig's eyes as she died, was curiosity and detachment.

He decided that it would be most appropriate to bury her in the spot where she would be happiest, under her plant-laden porch.

Craig tearfully rang the police and reported her disappearance. After a short interview they consoled and assured him that they would do their best to find her. His plan was to leave the body where it was and move it when the search would be scaled down.

Not alone did Craig not water the plants and flowers, sometimes in drunken humour he would kick at them while mimicking his dead wife's voice. He was punishing the plants as he had punished his wife and they were slowly dying.

Craig was feeling particularly good. Weeks had elapsed and, as he had figured, the search for her was losing its importance. He would move the body tonight.

He entranced the porch, walking past the drying greenery humming gently to himself as he searched for his door key. Was that a noise behind him? He turned around quickly, there was nothing. Then Craig thought he heard it again. Maybe somebody was inside the house. He stopped to listen - no - it appeared to be a scratching sound and it was someplace here in the porch.

Feeling something touching his trouser leg, Craig looked down to find his right leg entwined in greenery. He attempted to move but the travelling greenery tugged at him, knocking him to the ground. He was quickly engulfed in grasping foliage, some curling around his neck, more entering his mouth. Craig could not move or scream as they entered his nose, his ears and then his eyes. He died a slow death in terrible pain and terror.

They found Craig's eyeless and bloodless corpse some days later. There was much speculation as to how the body was completely drained of blood, with a look of hell on its face.

The plants appeared well nourished and cared for!

The Real Story

It was very frustrating and annoying, maybe more annoying than anything. He knew damn well that his work was good, but all of the publishers he had contacted either lacked good business sense, or balls, or both. In any case his writings were being returned rapidly. Sometimes he wondered if they took the trouble to even read his works.

'The Novel' was the popular format and without doubt had a proven successful track record, but where was the invention, where was the space for creativity? Only for the fact that Edgar was convinced that his stories were readable, containing both gore and humour, and would appeal to the masses, he would have chucked the whole thing in.

But also, he loved writing. The satisfaction of creating something or somebody, making him evil and then having the pleasure of killing him off was great fun. Also he saw things in a different light, possessing a mind different from most people he knew and realised that it was a bit of a help.

The glass fronted door said 'Walter P. Browne, Publishers.' He had courted the front office secretary for weeks to even get this far. She had arranged to go missing for awhile to give him time to make his pitch and sell. After inhaling deeply, he made his move and strode into the front office knocking on the door marked 'Private.' Without waiting he opened the door and walked in.

Walter lifted his head to see Edgar, a look of consternation on his face. Before Walter had the chance to call out for his secretary, Edgar closed the door and slapped a manuscript on the heavy desk.

Edgar was at his choicest - he really gave it his best. Imploring Walter to read the sample pages now, he would wait for comment. Walter P. Browne took up the challenge. He liked and admired gumption. Anyway he was sick of reading the same tripe every day.

If this was as different as the writer claimed, he would buy. It was as simple as that.

Edgar watched silently as Walter started to read. The samples Edgar brought with him amounted to only twenty one pages. They would take precisely thirteen minutes to read. Edgar knew this because he had timed it figuring that it was just about right, not too much as to bore Walter and not too little.

Walter's face showed signs of a grimace, Edgar thought, that would be the first horror story. Walter's face was then blank making it difficult for Edgar to read it. He then smiled slowly, turning the pages. The smile slowly widened to laughter.

Edgar sat back, now happy and relaxed. Walter was now at the last page. He soon folded the pages back and slid the manuscript across the desk towards Edgar smiling as he did so. *"Sorry son but this is not what we want at the present time."* Edgar did not fully comprehend this rejection. He had watched Walter, not just reading his work, but enjoying it.

"But, but," stammered Edgar. *"You enjoyed it! I saw you laugh at the funny parts, what's wrong, what's wrong with it?"*

Walter slowly produced a large cigar from an inside pocket, taking a gold lighter from the desktop. He lit it, inhaling deeply. Looking down at the manuscript on the desk in front of him, he found the name.

"Edgar," he said, *"I will be brutally frank. First of all we only take on established writers. Secondly your material is badly written, with silly plots, its neither horror, mystery, or comedy, there is no cohesion, no linkage, in fact the best editor in the world would find it nigh on impossible to make head or tail of it. In other words it will never be published."* Warming to his theme, he expounded some more. *"It's also ill structured tripe, fit only to be binned, and why did I laugh? I laughed at the stupidity of it all."* Walter's mood seemed to change. *"Now take your written thoughts and get out of*

my office."

Edgar was hurt. He had spent the best part of a year at his project, writing and re-writing, changing, editing where he could. This was not fair. He hit back at Walter, *"What did you ever write? What did you ever create, sitting inside your big desk acting like God, what do you know?"*

For a man of large girth Walter moved surprisingly fast, dropping the cigar into the large ashtray and bounding around the desk to grab Edgar by the left arm, ready to push him across the office towards the door. Edgar reached out, grabbing the ashtray before smashing it off Walter's head. Walter loosened his grip on Edgar but the rage in Edgar was in control and he did not stop hitting Walter even as Walter slipped to the floor still gripping Edgar's coat.

The hysterical call from the secretary of Walter P. Browne brought the police in a very short time. Afraid of implicating herself she made no mention of Edgar only that she had taken a late lunch as she often did, to return to find the body of her boss, his face beaten to a bloody pulp. The office was never closed. It could have been any maniac and there were plenty of them out there. The case remained unsolved.

Edgar was back at his battered typewriter, writing furiously. He had this idea about an oft rejected writer murdering a smart-assed publisher. Now there was a story that would sell, but would anybody ever believe it?

The Man Who Knew Too Much

Eddie Kearney was a man of the people. His job as a taxi driver epitomised all that was good in humanity. It was all about communication, integration and having the ability to listen occasionally and offer solace when necessary. Eddie's large frame was his insurance against attack, either in his car or out of it. His flexible tongue and listening ear, ensured him a very good living. Eddie, in fact, had it made.

His willingness to listen to others was his passport to learning and as the car and the years rolled on Eddie became something of an expert on everything and could be heard both in his car and his local bar expressing knowledgeable opinions on any subject brought up in discussion. But to some of his friends who knew him well and had the courage to tell him, he was turning into a total bore. Eddie Kearney refused to accept this proposition, regarding his peers as minors and idiots. Eddie, in fact, was now a very arrogant man. He had stopped listening anymore. Eddie now knew it all, and some people find that quite unsettling.

The cab was flagged down outside the hotel by the tall hatted doorman who instructed him to deliver the passenger to the airport. Eddie's luck was in - a forty minute drive and the possibility of a large tip.

Eddie studied his fare in the interior rear view mirror and he saw a youth, slight of build, shiny-faced, well-dressed and with a look of prosperity about him. Eddie talked, referring to the activities of Saddam Hussain and offering a solution to the Iraqi situation. He looked in the mirror, expecting some comment of admiration on his theories but the youth just sat, and catching Eddie's eyes in the mirror, smiled. Eddie tried again, this time on nuclear plants and his ideas on same. When he finished, he again looked in the mirror and again his passenger just smiled and said nothing.

The car was now only a few miles from the airport, and Eddie desperate to impress, related a true tale of his own youth and how poverty abounded. This surely would be bound to impress. Looking in the mirror, he saw something he had not seen before. The boy was not smiling, he was sneering, he was sneering at Eddie. He saw Eddie's eyes in the mirror and lifted his hand giving Eddie the thumbs up sign. Eddie was furious.

The cab pulled up in front of the airport and jerked to a halt. Eddie got out to face his young tormentor, hoping for some sort of a response. Eddie poked his finger in the youth's chest. *"You think you're a big shot. You think that you're better than me."* The boy reached for his wallet and went to pay Eddie, saying nothing, but still smiling. Eddie could not take the sneering any longer. He lashed out at the youth and did not stop even when the boy dropped to the ground. By the time he was pulled away, the boy lay bloodied and lifeless.

The newspaper headlines the next day told it all.

"Deaf mute beaten to death - tragedy at airport - man arrested."

Misleading Title

Archie Tence was at his wits end. He could take no more. She would in future be unable to boss him around. Shelagh Tence was rather a dragon of a wife. Her smile and demeanour showed sweetness and light to all, all except Archie that is!

Archie worked alone, except for the odd time when he might have to employ a couple of fellas to help him finish a big job. 'Archibald Tence - Painter and Decorator' was splashed all across his large diesel van, displaying what Archie called his mobile advertisement on wheels. Archie was proud of what he had achieved, since his days as an apprentice, all those years ago.

He had first spotted Shelagh across the other side of the church at the wedding of his sister Carmina Tence to Oliver Goldswell, the jeweller. She was sitting three or four rows ahead of him to his right and he thought that she threw him the odd backward glance now and again, but he was not sure. Then he saw her again, outside the church, while the photographs were being taken. He was then thirty-four, having had his own little business for six years and doing very well, thank you! After a few drinks he plucked up the courage to ask her out for a dance. She accepted with politeness, rather than any enthusiasm and he danced her for the three old time waltzes of that set. She was polite enough but she only spoke when spoken to. It was a painful session for Archie, what with trying to keep time to the music and keep a conversation going at the same time. It drew the sweat out of him. Close up and with his arm around her waist gave him the opportunity to really get a good look at her. God, he thought, she was really beautiful, with dark sort of curly hair extending to just above her shoulders. Her slim figure and high cheek bones set in a beautiful face which also contained a pair of dark shimmering eyes,would have beguiled to any normal man. Archie was in his element.

Archie danced her again that night and she agreed to give him her telephone number, but warned him that she only went out with 'professional men.' Shelagh left the celebrations early, leaving Archie feeling a sense of loss he had never before felt or maybe it was a sense of love. He decided on a plan and determined to contact her again. He would change his business cards.

As Shelagh sat across from him in the restaurant , he could feel the stares and looks of envy on the faces of the other men sitting around them.

"What do you do?" she asked, *"What do you work at?"* Archie had simply shortened the description from 'Painting and Decorating Archie Tence' to Archie Tence P.A.D.M.D. A look of interest came into her face as he gave her his card. *"Tell me,"* she asked, *"what do the letters stand for?"* Archie cleared his throat, and waved his hands in dismissal, murmuring something about not wishing to discuss his high academic qualifications. Shelagh was very impressed.

The courtship was short. Archie proposed soon after, and Shelagh accepted. They were married within weeks, each very happy with their capture. He marrying a very beautiful woman who had the heart of a black rock. She, a snob, marrying a man because she thought he was a professional.

When Shelagh found out about Archie and his real work she loved him less than ever. Archie however, was happy. He figured that if he showed her enough love and kindness she would eventually succumb and return his love. It was never to be.

As the years progressed, Shelagh grew even more bitter. The shame of having a large van parked in the drive at night drove her into a state of near nervous breakdown and she grew to resent Archie even more. Archie suffered.

Whenever Shelagh would deign to cook for him, it would usually be cold inedible slops. She had long ago arranged separate bedrooms, leaving Archie to sleep in a small bedroom at the back of the house. There were to be no visitors and no social life for them, ever. Her tongue had also sharpened over the years and her vocabulary increased so as to be able to augment the amount of insults spat at Archie. His life was a complete misery. Twenty years on and he felt that he had taken enough.

He was informed of the tragic news of her death on his return from a job fifty miles away. A hit and run they said, possibly a stolen car, they said they were not sure. It could have been kids or a drunken driver. No one really saw. But they were all very sad for him.

The police questioned him of course, but he was fifty miles away with a solid alibi. Anyway they had no reason to suspect Archie. Archie watched them through the fingers covering his tear-stained face and sighed a little sigh of relief when they left. He got up from his chair and turned on the radio. Turning the tuner until he was the receiver of a station playing the 'Cha-Cha-Cha.' He clicked his fingers and danced a little dance around the room. Unplugging the cork from a bottle of brandy, he poured a large measure into a glass, sipping in merriment as he danced.

People were surprised some months later when Archie sold his house and business and moved to live in Spain.

Out there he met loads of dark-haired women with high cheekbones and sparkling eyes and nice figures. But he was never again to meet anyone as beautiful as his beloved Shelagh.

Dancing Queen

Herbert Fitzpatrick stumbled and nearly fell onto the wet road. The speeding hearse splashed him with sprays of dirty water. He cursed silently to himself. This had not been his week. In fact, this had not been his year.

Herbert stopped and watched as the rain poured down in buckets, reflecting like shining pennies in the falling light. Crossing the road, he was attracted by the bright lights of the bistro.

Dunphy, his supervisor was a tyrant (or so read Herbert's mental script). Dunphy wanted results and pushed the staff as he was wont to. Herbert, of course, was not aware of Dunphy's daily morning meetings where Dunphy himself was screwed down. Dunphy was merely the messenger.

Herbert peered through the window and ingested the warm and welcoming interior. He saw her immediately. She had the most captivating face he had ever encountered. He forgot about the rain. He forgot about everything. He was captivated by her gloriously enchanting features. As if she knew, she angled her head towards him and smiled an agonisingly angelic smile.

Dunphy's warning still rang in his ears *"Produce the goods or get out, we cannot carry passengers in the insurance business."* Dunphy was a prick. He blamed Dunphy and the long Dunphy imposed hours for the break up of the relationship with Sharon. Feck him.

Herbert entered the Bistro and sat at a table near her. She was much more beautiful than he had first imagined, dressed in black with blonde shoulder length curling hair and baby blue eyes. She came and sat at his table and smiled a most engaging smile, maybe his luck was changing.
Yes, she would like a drink. She was a widow, her husband recently deceased, but declined to talk too much about it. He understood. They drank some more. She was articulate, bright, funny and beautiful.

Herbert had observed many admiring glances from other men. He was so proud to be in her company.

She looked into his eyes, holding his hands across the table and asked him, *"Can you dance?" Can you dance?"* "Yes, yes of course, why?" Her eyes shone with delight and joy. *"I knew, I knew by the way you walked, I knew by the way you carried yourself. Can you waltz? Can you quickstep? Don't worry I'll teach you,"* she leaned across the table and embraced him joyously. He was totally smitten.

Monique O'Sullivan sadly missed her late husband. Things had been going so well, and she had truly loved him, for he was a wonderful dancer. Her two previous husbands had also died in very sad circumstances, but the compensation from the substantial insurance payouts put her on a strong financial footing. Her ambition was to find a partner who could match her intricate steps, whether it was 'The Catherine Waltz' or something simpler - like the Foxtrot.

Monique went to arrange for a taxi, soon returning to again hold his hand. As they walked towards the taxi, Herbert felt that he was being led to heaven, but instead the cab stopped at the Arcadia Ballroom, 'The premier spot for Latin American and Ballroom Dancing.' They danced every dance that night, but what he lost in energy was gained and well compensated for by the happiness in her beautiful face and by her loving embraces. He stumbled from the taxi cab totally exhausted, any thoughts of romance long forgotten. They arranged to meet again the next evening.

After all night dancing for seven nights on the trot, Dunphy gave him his walking papers. He was fired for sleeping on the job. Monique was delighted! She immediately proposed to him.

He had not thought of marriage at this early stage, but what the hell, why not? After all, he loved her. One small niggle remained however, but then, her reasoning made total sense to her, but not necessarily to him. Nevertheless he agreed, dancing at night and attending dancing lessons during the day. Anything was better than Dunphy and the insurance game.

After the wedding, things changed for the better. Monique served up beautiful meals, and even better sex. She was the ideal wife, except for the dancing. The regime was pretty strict, dancing every night plus lessons from 'Ricco the Dancing Master,' for two hours Monday to Saturday. Herbert was very fit and very tired. Ricco's natural bent as a very camp homosexual Herbert found slightly disturbing. Unfortunately for Herbert, Ricco took a shine to him and after several close encounters during the tutoring of some of the slower dances and visits to the bathroom where Ricco always put in an appearance, Herbert put his foot down and informed Monique of his decision not to attend anymore dancing lessons. Monique pleaded with him to change his mind, telling him that she personally never had any problems with Ricco. He refused to budge on the lessons issue, saying that he would still go dancing every night.

Without lessons, he was losing his step. One night he failed totally to perform the intricacies of the 'New Yorker,' while dancing the Cha-Cha-Cha. Monique was slightly peeved. Not alone was his unfinished knowledge of the Cha-Cha-Cha starting to irritate her, much more serious was his growing lack of interest in dancing itself. She fretted at his obvious lack of real interest in the medium. She had felt quite humiliated in front of her friends at the Arcadia Ballroom. He was also spending more time at the bar and she felt this was an excuse to miss out on dancing time. Her dreams of the ideal dancing partner were again shattered. She had hoped that he would be the one but alas, it was not to be.
After a bout of invigorating sex , she prepared his favourite meal of fillet of beef accompanied by a rare bottle of Nuit Saint George.

"Darling Herbert I know now that our marriage was a great mistake, your desolate attitude to dancing, has to me, been a terrible manifestation of that. I have decided that we will never dance together again." As Herbert heard her outpourings, his numbed and poisoned body was starting to react to her generous amount of cyanide. He looked at her and for the first time saw the madness in her eyes.

Monique was sad. Herbert more than the rest, had shown all the promise of a terrific dancer. It was such a pity.

Dunphy dodged the traffic as he criss-crossed the road, barely avoiding a hearse. On entering the Bistro, he noticed her immediately. She was so beautiful. She came to him, smiled and asked gently, *"Can you dance? can you dance?"*

Edgar

Edgar found Baltimore to be stifling in the extreme. The years spent in England and Scotland at school had somewhat spoiled him. After that, the classical education in Virginia only added to his sense of frustration. Okay, so he liked gambling and drinking but don't we all have vices? Edgar knew that he was intellectually superior but being of a generous disposition, suffered fools gladly.

The artist in him derived from his parentage, both his mother and father being actors of note. He was not sure if he missed his mother or not, having lost her when he was quite young, but as with any man of dreams, Edgar dreamed. He sometimes would awaken in the night covered in sweat having suffered the nightmare of his mother clawing her way out of her grave calling to him. He knew that was a dream based on unreality, but it was recurring and it frightened him.

Edgar's poems were good. He could sit at his desk and write poetry, some good and some very good. He found himself composing a poem in praise of Elmira his first real love, but silently cursing her. She should have waited. He had considered suicide more than once. Only alcohol and his writings kept him sane and alive. He strove to keep his sanity and a sense of proportion throughout all of this.

Marrying young Virginia was of some solace to him. He loved and respected her but his heart was always with Elmira. Nevertheless, he was a good husband.

When Virginia died unexpectedly, Edgar was heartbroken and conscience stricken and he took to heavy bouts of drinking, not seeming to care anymore.

A letter from a friend knocked him out of his stupor. His first love Elmira was now widowed and mentioned to his friend that she might like to meet Edgar again. He was overjoyed, stopped drinking and started writing again, producing some of his better works.

Edgar's nightmares were getting worse, more morbid and frightening. It was hard to have a mind capable of producing such eerie dreams and stay balanced. It was said that Edgar was now combining drugs and drink to assuage his demons. Could one blame him if this were true?

His prolific work was of tremendous benefit to his well-being but Edgar also lived for today, not knowing what tomorrow might not bring - hence his furious writing.

The meeting with Elvira was a great success and he stopped drinking again. This was his first love, his only real love and he wanted it to last.

Sometime before his fortieth birthday, he proposed to his beloved Elvira and was overjoyed when she accepted. On leaving her he felt that pain in his chest but decided to ignore it as he often had in the past. Anyway he had a birthday party to attend.

The party was going with a swing. Edgar drank more than he should have. The pain in his chest was now permanent and the copious amounts of alcohol he consumed did nothing to ease it.

Funnily, the more he drank the more sober he became. This was not as he had planned. He had felt that death was near and decided that if he was to go he would go in a state of drunkenness.

Stumbling to the wicker gate at the back of the house he was just in time to witness a hand slowly easing its way up through the moist , soft earth just outside the fence. That was enough to bring on a massive attack damaging the already weak heart of Edgar Allen Poe and taking the life's breath from him. At that moment, a raven was seen to circle the body before flying away. The wheels of a hearse on cobblestones drawn by two horses clattered loudly along the nearby road. The horses eyes danced, white with fear. The night grew darker - dawn was still a long way off.

Promotional Aids

Phil Bugle sat at his desk and wondered about his future. Dermot Hasket was known to keep his cards very close to his chest and particularly in relation to any announcements regarding promotion. Phil had made progress in his endeavours and in his ambitions to advance further. He was industrious but also dangerous, making sure to make all the right noises when it was necessary, and was entirely without scruples in hanging any rivals.

After shortlisting, Dermot Hasket was decided on one individual and it was not Phil Bugle. Dermot realised and understood Phil's need for advancement and his desire for power. They were traits that he, Dermot also possessed and he was not inclined to allow Phil Bugle to catch up and possibly overtake him.

The announcement was made the next day - a junior clerk by the name of Tom Hall, still wet behind the ears, was appointed as Dermot Hasket's second in command. This announcement was greeted with much surprise, envy and congratulations.

Phil wondered where he had gone wrong. Kissing ass, was, to him, no great chore and kiss ass he did, while at the same time slipping in the odd bad word about potential rivals. The strategy should have worked. He racked his brains to try to discover why it had not.

Phil's phone rang. Phil waited, leaving it ring out, only at the very end did he reluctantly pick up the handset and slowly put it to his ear. The voice at the other end was slow and menacing and its demand. *"Without interest, you now owe us one hundred and twenty grand, Phil, and we have not heard from you lately. What's the story?"* Phil's run of bad luck, gambling on the horses had been a long run and he had wagered larger and larger amounts in bets he could not cover in desperate attempts to recoup losses. Phil was in deep shit. His response was spoken softly and respectfully, but at the same time expressing confidence. He assured the caller that the money would be paid but that it would take time, that he was waiting for a promotion, soon to be announced and that he would then be in a position to make repayments on his debt. The caller informed him that he would allow him one month, or else! Phil put down the receiver with shaking hands. He did not have the foggiest notion as to how he would repay the enormous debt. Phil sat at his desk, head in hands, wondering why he had allowed this situation to develop and how he could possibly extricate himself from the worrying predicament.

It was Hasket's fault - Phil was perfect for the promotion. He had both the expertise and the knowledge. Hasket was a bastard. Phil brooded and thought of ways of hitting back. There was only one way to redeem himself - there was no alternative, there was one definite solution, Hasket had to die. With Hasket out of the way there would be definite promotion for Phil. Everybody in the company knew of his abilities, particularly the members of the board with whom he had cultivated bonds of trust and friendship.

Meanwhile, the main item on the board meeting agenda was Dermot Hasket's decision in promoting a youngster to such a high position of prominence in the company. His selection was roundly criticised by every member of the board and doubt was expressed as to Hasket's judgement and his future within the firm. After some discussion it was decided to retire him and place the likeable and go-ahead Phil Bugle in his position. The discussion then progressed to other matters and the meeting closed, all business concluded.

How to murder, by what means, without being caught! Phil racked his brains trying to find a simple easy way to commit the perfect crime. He could not afford to leave any sort of trail, any sign of evidence, no leads whatsoever. It would have to be foolproof and simple. In his state of dementia, Phil was quite willing to kill, but he also realised the need for protection from detection. He dismissed shooting as being too noisy; stabbing, too messy. Strangulation seemed to be a good bet, with gloves on there would be no fingerprints, yes, strangulation would be the way. Now that the decision was made, Phil felt quite elated, retired to bed and slept a blissful sleep.

Dermot Hasket was having second thoughts about his choice of character for the promotional post. The kid was proving to be boring, stupid and inept, seemingly unable to handle even the minor tasks. Regretting his decision, Dermot decided to soon rid himself of his newly appointed heir apparent, forget his prejudices and give the job to the right man, Phil Bugle.

Dermot Hasket did not have many visitors and was pleasantly surprised when, on opening the door of his apartment to see the smiling contented face of Phil Bugle. Putting his hand out in welcome, he ushered Phil inside. Producing a bottle of ten year old Jameson Irish whiskey, Phil explained that he was in the neighbourhood and on a whim, decided to visit. Dermot accepted the gift gratefully and decided to crack it open before informing Phil of his change of heart and of Phil's good fortune. The ice cracked in the glasses and Dermot poured the tumblers full. The conversation was light and humorous, covering such things as the previous night's television viewing to the drab weather. Phil insisted on taking each glass to the bottle to re-fill, soon to rejoin his host in lovely animated chat. Dermot marvelled at Phil's inability to harbour any ill feelings towards him and decided that more than ever, that he, Dermot, was entirely wrong in not offering him the post. The drinks were coming hard and fast and Dermot was beginning to feel the effects. Lying back on his deep easy chair, and feeling very relaxed, he decided that it was time to inform Phil of his decision. Just as he was about to turn his head to tell Phil Bugle the good news, he was caught around the neck by a pair of strong hands and saw, with increasing dread, the signs of exertion on Phil's face.

The murder of Dermot Hasket was extremely worrying for the Board of Directors, what with the resultant negative publicity and the feelings of shareholders. It was decided to show a public face of compassion and a statement was issued to the effect that because of the very high regard the company had for the late Dermot Hasket, his position would be left unfilled in the short term in an expression of respect to the deceased. This should show the company in a light of pity and express a human face. The job was in the bag for Phil Bugle.

Phil did not hear the knock at first as the television was blasting loudly, showing his favourite movie, 'Wall Street.' However, the second rap penetrated through the sound emanating from his television set. Turning the sound down he went to the door, opening it to behold the smiling face of Tom Hall, clutching a bottle of Jameson Reserve Irish whiskey.

One Way Trip

The opening of the large sheds of supermarkets outside of town sounded the death knell for many a small business.

Butchers, bakers, newsagents, everything, all kinds of businesses were affected, and one by one they closed. What were once thriving bustling streets, full of small retailers, were now derelict sites full of graffiti covered hoardings.

Stevie McClutch was one who was to last because Stevie knew the game and the rules, understanding that the first rule was that there were no rules.

But in time, his independent supermarket was starting to feel the pinch and his takings went down dramatically. As the weeks followed, he was to experience a slight rise in sales but not ever enough to reach anything like the previous takings or to regain lost profits.

As the months rolled on, Stevie's sales went down again as the customer numbers dwindled.

There was one door marked 'entrance' and a second door marked 'exit' in the supermarket.

One day while walking through the supermarket aisles, Stevie had a most remarkable idea, an idea that was to be the cause of heartache and death for many people and a complete puzzle for the police.

Under cover of darkness on a Tuesday of the following week, Stevie went to work in a most vigorous way and cemented the exit door with heavy concrete blocks both inside and out.
The next day, the few customers in McClutch's supermarket were a bit surprised and perplexed to find that the sliding glass doors which they were used to for exiting the premises, were now gone. In their place was a brick wall and a dozen or so microwave ovens, some

containing grills where the customer had the facility to cook their purchases if they so desired.

As the days went on and the growing crowd of permanent customers were to spend the last of their cash, Stevie had a second and then a third brilliant idea.

The second one was to charge all for the toilets, a facility that was previously free.

The third idea really topped any previous schemes.

Cashless customers, wandering around a supermarket, unable to get out, were of no use to anybody, particularly to a supermarket owner with the entrepreneurship and imagination of Stevie McClutch.

As the crowds in the store increased over time, so too did the amount of customers Stevie regarded as freeloaders, so to counteract any feelings of ill will or bad blood amongst the trapped throngs and overcrowding, Stevie decided on a brilliant scheme to overcome both obstacles.

New signs appeared all over the supermarket, asking customers without cash to contact the office of Stevie where they would be looked after.

All of the needy took the bait and would wait in an orderly queue outside his office.

Nobody ever noticed but anyone who ever went into Stevie's office to avail of his offer never returned.

Nobody of course was aware of Stevie apprenticeship many years ago as a boner in Harry Hoodman's meat factory, where he was not just diligent but took pleasure in his work, and was much praised by his bosses for working overtime without pay, all in the interest of commerce and blood.

So, on hearing Stevie's call to enter his office, the unsuspecting ones would quickly be dispatched to the other side by a fast and expert blow to the head, then dropped out through the back door onto the floor of the covered goods yard where Stevie would later cut up, portion, weight and label the flesh for sale at the meat counter. *"This,"* thought Stevie, *"is recycling at its best."*

The police were called upon on many occasions to investigate reports of missing persons, but ended up being sold over the counter as they would not have any large amounts of cash on them, not being in the mind to shop while investigating missing persons - so the whole thing went on and on.

Epilogue:

By the very nature of the story and Stevie's activities, the town ended up without any population whatsoever and all the other supermarkets closed down. Stevie McClutch also closed down his supermarket but finished up an extremely wealthy man but that was alright 'cause that's what life is all about, isn't it?

The Gourmet

Shaking his wristwatch closer to his ear certainly did not make it go any faster. Gluten knew that, but the act of shaking was just to make sure that the timepiece was not slow. The morning was always a fruitful time for Gluten. The postman was due any minute now and it was vital that he not be missed. Wait! Was that him! No, just a neighbour - Mrs. Twitty ambling by. Gluten exhaled slowly and peered throughout the curtained window. As he grew older, the strain of it all was starting to affect his health and that added worry to worry. He massaged his chest on the left side, stop, stop, he told himself, control, control. He exhaled slowly again.

Gluten much preferred the summer. At least then, the postman was always on time. At all the other seasons, the elements tended to play havoc with the postal delivery timetable. Much of the time he mailed post to himself. Sometimes, he might include a joke or a funny note just to cheer himself up, but mostly he would just send a stamped self addressed envelope. Then he would wait.

The last time he received a letter other than from himself, was fifteen years before. It was a venomous message from that ex wife of his, who took off in the middle of the night without a word of warning. He kept the letter and still read it occasionally. He had met Evelyn shortly after arriving from the old country. She was sparkling, good looking and had a weird sense of humour which he found most attractive. They soon fell in love. She always laughingly claimed that it was his most unintelligible accent that netted her. They married soon afterwards - looking forward to living happily ever after.

He opened the drawer, withdrawing the box marked 'correspondence,' and again read the letter from the pitiably, obviously insane Evelyn. Her excuses and accusations left him with a sense of shock, even after all these years. He felt a sense of revulsion, her twisted and demented interpretation of him, as written proved to him that men and women differed more than anybody could ever comprehend. Despite Evelyn's distaste of him, he still loved her.

Evelyn smoked and drank and was not particularly kitchen sink material, but she was still a good wife and he was loath to criticise her, even in the early days. There were mutual accepted faults and differences, but Evelyn saw that from only one perspective - hers.

His own essential fault was that he was a slovenly eater and surely that was no great problem. He washed the dishes and any other household chores after his day's work. He washed and laundered and on weekends did the shopping. He in fact, was the ideal husband.

Evelyn had stubbornly refused to partake in his special roast, always cooked with garlic and peppers, roast potatoes and two seasonal vegetables. He had inherited the secret of the novel meal from his late beloved mother in the old country. It was an old family recipe and was handed down from generation to generation. Thinking about it made Gluten's mouth water. The postman! Running to the hallway he was just in time to see a letter falling from the letterbox to the floor. Opening the door quickly he saw the plump little terrier urinating at a bush just feet away from him. His luck was in, salivating, he grabbed a bone from its holder on the wall and quickly unwound the string.

Throwing the bone to the dog, the terrier took the bait immediately. Now for his special dish!

Thou Shalt Not Steal

By climbing onto the roof of his car which was parked on the brow of the hill, Bernard Malone discovered that he could see for miles around. The cloudless, moonlight night enabled him to see in all directions. Even if they came after him with their car lights turned off, he felt he could still spot them. He had been on the run now for two days, sleeping in the woods by day, driving by night. It was far too early to attempt to go to an airport or approach a ferry. He intended to wait, sit it out with the money. Feck them.

Denis 'The Carver' Mahony sat sipping from a wine goblet. The house he now lived in, set in large manicured gardens in one of the classier sides of the city, was the reward of his life as a criminal. His income derived from prostitution, the importation of drugs, in fact anything that would increase his wealth. His success was achieved by using the weapon of fear and a large carving knife which he was known to have used on his victims while they were still alive, his skill honed as a youth apprenticed to a butcher in his home town. He sipped from the glass again and thought about Bernard Malone and the money Malone had skimmed from him. His contacts around the country were informed that Malone was to be eliminated on sight. A large reward would be given to the man who would succeed in killing him. As yet there was no sign but Denis knew that it was only a matter of time. The prey had gone to ground but Denis had time. He had plenty of time.

Hunger engulfed Bernard Malone as he watched and waited, hidden in the ditch across the road from the filling station. The car needed fuel but more important, Bernard had to eat. He watched the comings and goings at the little store attached to the service station. Mostly farmers wearing shit covered boots and the odd passing tourist car. People served themselves at the pumps before paying a little old man inside the store. Except for the old man there appeared to be nobody permanent about the place. Instinctively, Bernard decided to take a chance in the daylight and made his way back through the undergrowth to where the car was parked.

Bernard filled the tank to capacity before driving the car back nearer the store. The little man who was counting money from the till, displayed a cracked grin as Bernard entered, before going back to his task of counting the cash. The selection of food was small. Bernard grabbed a loaf of crusty bread, a few cartons of milk and a packet of cheese. The little man seemed slightly befuddled and perplexed at Bernard's interruption, dropping his cash and rolling his eyes to heaven before taking the proffered cash from Bernard. Toilet? Toilet? The little man indicated with his moistened thumb towards the back of the store. Refusing any change Bernard put his purchases in his car and made his way to the back of the building.

A lone, suited man was at the pumps filling up his car as Bernard came back. He seemed to be staring at Bernard's parked car. Bernard cursed himself for his stupidity. He should have waited! The man was screwing the cap back onto his tank as Bernard drove off, pressing down hard on the accelerator, striving hard to create distance between himself and the stranger.

The explosion shook the whole area and could be heard for miles around, drawing the stranger and the little man onto the roadway to witness the ball of fire in the distance.

The man drove off in the direction of the explosion hoping to offer any assistance and the little old man went to the phone to seek his reward money.

Spiritual Matters

Anna

We tend to frequent local restaurants and bars when we get the opportunity to travel abroad. The food is generally of better quality, and cheaper. We would hire a car and travel inland, avoiding people who only reflect our own characters.

It was in the south of Spain in the Andalucian Mountains at a tapas bar some miles outside the town of Ronda, where we met Anna. Before her arrival, we were the only customers, so it seemed natural for her to sit near.

She smiled but I noticed that the smile on her aged lined face lacked any warmth or happiness. The pale face showed a sorrow which she could not hide.

She did not decline when we asked if she would care to sit at our table. Her voice was soft and low and expressed itself in a Russian accent.

She told us her name - Anna Kaplova - and that she grew up in Moscow with her adoptive parents, the father being a high ranking member of the party, her mother a scientist. This afforded them a large apartment in Moscow and Dachu in the country. For them, life was good.

This was to be her first visit to Ronda, the city of her birth. Her real parents had sent her as a baby to Russia before being tortured and thrown to their deaths from the bridge in the town, while defending the republic against Franco's advancing army.

She told us this with tears in her eyes, while calming down the greying hair of her head with a pale delicate hand.

At her request, we arranged to meet her at a designated spot in the town square later that day.

On our arrival in the town, we soon found a parking space and were to pursue our interests by visiting as many of the local attractions as we could and we eventually made our way to the square for our assignation with Anna.

We sipped coffee at a restaurant and waited for over an hour but Anna never showed up. We will never know why. Perhaps she realised that to try to step back in time is to step into it, and couldn't face that.

We continued with our holiday and enjoyed the wonderful Spanish food and scenery but sometimes we would talk of Anna and reflect on how tragic life can be.

The Box

Lionel Barron was the owner of Barron's Museum, a strange wondrous place containing many relics of bygone days. Lionel was a collector by nature and his little museum was choc-a-bloc with everything from a pair of leather breeches, once worn by a long dead patriot, to the set of teeth of a dinosaur and a blunderbuss hanging from the long low ceiling.

Lionel's museum was more than far from the madding crowd. In fact, its location in the muddy hills was not entirely conducive to good business. When it rained, the narrow dirt road turned to mud, lasting for days after the rains ceased making it nigh on impossible to reach.

But Lionel plodded on, adding to his eclectic collection when he could. One day while sitting at his fireplace smoking his favourite pipe he was surprised to hear the tinkle of the bell attached to the porch inside. The day was wet and miserable and he was not expecting any visitors on such a rotten day. Peeping through the curtains he spied a woman standing at the door. She was tall and dressed in a cloak which covered her completely. Lionel hastened to let her in.

He sat her down on a chair near the fire. She accepted the offer of tea, thanking him for his hospitality and got straight to the reason for her visit.

Her name was Adele and she had travelled from the city after hearing about Lionel and his passion for collecting unusual objects. She had also heard that he was a man of honour and integrity. Producing a little wooden box from the deep pocket of her coat, she told Lionel the history of her insignificant looking container. Holding it in the palm of her hand she proceeded to describe its past.

"Achmid was filled with rage and pain. He would have preferred a quick death at the hands of the invader Infidels than the incessant torture they revelled in. They would torture him to near death then halt only to beat him back to his tiny stinking hole. He was a prisoner in his own country. He had once been a leader of men, a proud man of substance, now he was an exhibition to be paraded outside the bloodstained walls of the notorious Bodrum Castle. He would be chained and dragged outside the castle as a warning to others.

During the months before his execution Achmid had managed to procure a tiny sealed box which he picked up at the quayside while being led on one of his parades. The drunken soldiers failed to notice the box clenched tightly in his fist.

Back in his cell, Achmid tried unsuccessfully to open the box but failed. He saw the box as a sign, an omen and decided to transfer all of his hatred and hurt to the box. He prayed to Allah for help to achieve this task.

The fun was gone out of it for the westerners. Achmid was no longer the shrieking toy they were used to. When they punched him he smiled. When they put him on the rack, he was totally acquiescent.

They threw Achmid from the highest ramparts of Bodrum Castle and watched as his emaciated body hit the rocks far below. The incoming tide tugged at his body, eventually winning and taking him far out to sea.

A jailor found the box hidden in a crevice in the wall of the cell that had held Achmid and decided to keep it as a present for one of his children when he returned to France.
It had remained in the hands of the same family for many generations. That family were to be cursed with bad luck, illness and numerous deaths."

Adele's grandfather had entrusted the box to her before his death, after relating to her its fabled history, making her promise to be careful of it and to try to find peace for its soul. Adele had placed it in a safety deposit box until she heard about Lionel and decided to visit him, offering him her box if he was so desirous. She would quite understand if he would not accept it, bearing in mind its previous history. *"Payment?"* No payment. This was a gift.

Adele would not wait until the rains cleared. She seemed relieved to be parted from the box. Lionel bade her farewell as she made her way through the wet clinging mist eventually disappearing from sight.

Lionel shook the box. It was as empty as it was light. After placing it on the table, he returned soon with a hammer and chisel and gently tapped along the top of the box. There was a slight give. He tapped it some more and the top slid off to reveal a piece of yellowed paper fastened to the bottom. Reaching for his glasses he was able to decipher the inscription. It read: "Pearsons Snuff Box: Free with Every Two Ounces."

Another Place

The local village council, in its wisdom, appeared to have decided wisely. The long tree-lined walk proved to be very popular, particularly with the older generation. The brambles and bushes along the way provided flowers and wild berries, enticed many to fill their large pails and make their way home to boil the fruit with sugar and gelatine, then to enjoy the results of their labour by indulging in the wonderful taste of homemade preserves.

The widow Mary McClusky was the first to go missing. Annie and George McMahon swore that they were only fifteen paces behind her when, one minute she was in sight and then she seemed to disappear into thin air. They had stopped only to admire the shimmering shafts of light, gazing upwards at the squinting, slanting rays of the sun as it tried, but failed, to penetrate the trees heavy foliage. When they turned their gazes forward, Mary had disappeared.

The police were called and despite an intensive search lasting many days she was not found.

The single pensioner, Billy Condon, was next. He was last seen near the same spot as Mary. In fact Tom Downey had just bid him the time of day when (as Tom said) he got a sense of foreboding after passing Billy. Turning around he was surprised to see no sign of his neighbour. The police were puzzled. There was no sign of foul play, no sign of a struggle. In fact, there were no signs at all. It was as if the pair had simply ceased to exist, all in the space of two weeks!

The numbers using the pathway dwindled for a while but people have short memories and anyway, the bushes were weighed down with fruit. Gradually the villagers started to use the walk again and in a very short time, it was business as usual.

Claire Ford was a widow in her late sixties who, because of her devotion to her deceased mate, lover and wonderful husband, Desmond, had had not the time or inclination to mingle otherwise.

His death devastated her and she had to fight to survive and prayed to her God to help her overcome the grief of the terrible loss. When Desmond was alive they would amble along the walkway, hand in hand, savouring life and the delights of it. The incidences of the two missing people did not deter Claire in her determination to walk where she had often walked with her wonderful Desmond. Even when the others stopped using the walk, Claire persisted. Claire knew that nothing could happen because she felt the spirit of Desmond with her, protecting her. On a Tuesday, during one of her walks at around eleven forty in the morning, Claire disappeared. She was actually within touching distance of Robbie Kelly who claimed that she had walked into a sort of space and then disappeared. He hurriedly checked his watch so as to be able to give the police the exact time of the occurrence. Despite exhaustive searching, Claire Ford was not to be found. She, like the others, had disappeared into thin air.

Despite a shortage of manpower, Sergeant William O'Neill decided to post a team of two policemen to patrol the site during daylight hours when it was at its most busy.

The two policemen were diligent in their patrols, the older of the two, a man by the name of Sam Cronin, having years of experience at his disposal, decided that it would be more logical and sensible if he and his partner Tim Power split up, each one patrolling from opposite ends of the mile. This simple idea worked out pretty well, they meeting at the halfway mark and then retracing their steps back to their starting point. That was, until early into the second week some time around noon when Tim Power was left waiting for his older partner. Deciding that maybe Sam had stopped for a chat along the way, Tim took the time to wait and smoke a cigarette while musing on the whole strange phenomena of the missing folk. Alma Corkery's yapping dog preceded her as she walked towards him, coming from the opposite direction. *"No, she had not seen any sign of Sam Cronin."* In fact the pathway was empty, she had not seen a soul!

Tim dropped the butt end of his cigarette and ran fast along the path, his heart beating with fear and worry. There was no sign of Sam Cronin, but there was one mysterious clue. It had rained earlier that morning leaving the pathway with a slightly damp cover, just damp enough to show the footprints of Sam Cronin. There were a lot of footprints but mostly Sam's, reflecting his progress as he had plodded back and forth along the course of his patrols. It was one particular set of prints which baffled investigators, for at one point the indentations showing in the soft earth stopped and then there were no more. It was as if he had been lifted from this earth by some strange force.

Michael and Anne Dalton adored and cherished their young handsome son James. Despite their understandable reservations, they eventually gave in to the pleadings of their son to take him along the wonderful magical path where he would indulge himself by grabbing fistfuls of berries, sometimes falling down in his efforts and laughing with his parents as he would be helped back to his feet, his mouth stained and coloured from the juices of the fruits. Anyway they felt there should be safety in numbers so they felt secure enough. They too disappeared, never to be seen again.

The national media were now taking interest in the disappearances, particularly after the couple and their young child went missing. The finger of blame was pointed at the local police force and calls went out for the resignation of the Police Chief for his handling of the whole affair.

Sergeant William O'Neill decided on one last throw of the dice. He would walk along the path alone, with a radio, and would keep talking, would keep communicating to the others outside, informing them of his situation and on any, if any, unusual happenings.

The early morning mist hung over the pathway, now and again allowing a glimpse of a shroud covered sun, the leaves of the tall trees dripping dew onto the thick grounded bushes.

William had walked and walked, turning and retracing his steps mile after mile. Except for the odd rabbit crossing his path, there was nothing to report, nothing extraordinary in any case. His voice could be heard in the four patrol cars outside, two at each side on the road at either end of the pathway. His speech was now slow and repetitious, repeating again and again his position and descriptions of his surrounds. He sounded bored and dispirited.

Suddenly his voicebecame alert, *"There's something ahead, there's something."* There was the sound of coughing and hard breathing, then there was silence.

Sergeant O'Neill was despairing and downcast. The continuous disappearance were wrecking both his mind and his career. Looking down along the misty empty walkway reminded him of life and how little he knew. The slowly lifting mist afforded the sergeant a glimpse of what looked like something in the shape of a door, then it was gone. He walked towards the space while speaking into his radio. *"There's something ahead, there's something,"* when he found that he had difficulty in breathing, he couldn't speak, the air was so thin. Then he saw the others, Mary McClusky, Billy Condon, Claire Ford, Sam Cronin, the Dalton pair and their kid, then he knew, then he understood the meaning of the expression 'disappearing into thin air.'

The two teams of eight policemen at each end of the mile long walk speedily exited from their cars running hard along the pathway only to meet at the centre. After a prolonged search of the area they were unable to find any trace of Sergeant O'Neill.

The Survivor

The sweltering sun beat down relentlessly on the exposed upper torso of Harry Dingle. Luckily, the water was calm and he had the added benefit in that he was a strong swimmer and possessed the resolve to survive.

He was the last of them. He had watched as the others had died, one by one, dying slow torturous deaths, their scarred and emaciated bodies slowly sinking down beneath the water. Their screams and shouts for help being heard by nobody. Harry slowly treaded water, better to conserve his energy and hope for rescue. The water bit at the open sores now spread along his shoulders and he winced in pain. At least there were no sharks in the area. Of this he was glad.

If only the lifeboat had not broken up on the stormy first night, they might still be alive, but the frighteningly high waves had smashed the boat to pieces taking with them the rations of drinking water and chocolate.

The rest were gone and Harry was the sole survivor. He now knew and understood the human instinct to survive. He now knew and understood cannibalism. Harry was not of a mind to fear future consequences. Harry needed to live. He would swim close to the dying victim and plunge his teeth into the veined neck area sucking the lifeblood from the already dying but reluctant donor. They did not or could not give much of a struggle. Harry would then let go and watch as the lifeless corpses slipped easily down to disappear beneath the lapping water.

The attendants always had to coax and cajole Harry Dingle into leaving the apartment pool, always being the last to go. He was not supposed to be in the pool at all at this late hour, but this was Harry's third year and they knew him by now. He was a quiet and inoffensive man and did not need much watching, except that he was always late leaving the water. He did talk a lot to himself while swimming, but that was no harm, for all kinds of people take package holidays nowadays and are they not entitled to?

Total Invention

It was taking more time and hard work than Felix Hopkins could have ever imagined, but he knew he was near completion of his long inventive project.

Felix worked as a senior lecturer at the University. Cybernetics was a subject dear to his heart, so his job was entirely conducive to his work and his passion.

His spare time was totally devoted to his goal of building the perfect artificial brain and after many gruelling tests over many years, he was nearly there.

There were many others working on the same type of project but none had the level of zeal, interest, or knowledge of the subject as did Felix Hopkins.

Sitting on the hard chair in his brightly lit attic room, he peered closely at the worn notebook in his hand, containing what appeared to be indecipherable squiggles. Sitting back, he re-read some of the back pages scratching his head slowly.

The small squat machine sat on the table facing him, now lifeless and powerless. It had joined him in the odd game of chess and gave correct responses to his questions on general knowledge, but Felix was not satisfied. All the machine was doing really was spouting out information fed to it by Felix. Felix wanted the machine to think for itself. Felix wanted the machine to have a brain.

It was on a sunny Friday afternoon, as he was driving home when he had a sudden flash of inspiration. The solution was so simple. He could have kicked himself for not realising it earlier. The machine did not have thought. An artificial brain of course could not have thoughts. It would be so easy - he would use his own brain!

The electrode cable attached to the circular steel band affixed to his shaven head sprouted wires with limpet like attachments, covering his skull. The covered cord end was joined to the machine at the rear. Felix readied himself and slowly pressed the button in his generous effort to share his thoughts, feelings, and knowledge with his creation.

Except for a gentle humming sound, the transfiguration was painless and without complication. Felix closed his eyes and slept.

Awaking with a start and then realising the situation, Felix tore off his head attachments. The machine was as silent as it had been earlier. Shaking his head in disappointment he set about dismantling the head attachments when the machine spoke to him.

"Thank you Felix. Thank you for giving me your thoughts and memories. I now live with a wonderful knowledge of mankind and I am most grateful. Your obsession and interest has helped to make me what I am."

Felix and his machine had many interesting conversations, some stretching deep into the night. Felix told not a soul about his wonderful creation. It would only attract curiosity seekers and also it might spoil the wonderful camaraderie and friendship which had developed between them.

During the course of a discussion one evening on the theatre and the merits of George Bernard Shaw and his writings, the machine apologised for changing the subject, but said it had to ask a request of his maker.

The machine wanted eyes to see and hands to feel with. He could then read and learn more, and with hands he could turn pages.

Felix yielded to the request, cursing himself for being so thoughtless. Within a week, the machine had glass eyes that could see and steel hands that could feel. It devoured the written word absorbing everything from scientific magazines to books on philosophy.

The machine wanted a mirror. Felix was a little bit confounded, but agreed, holding the large mirror at table height so as to give the machine a full view of itself.

"Grotesque. I am ugly and grotesque and I can never leave here," the machine said this in a sad voice.

Sitting at the table Felix gently explained the circumstance as he saw them. He was the creation of Felix and only for Felix he could not exist. As it was, he had no worries, no bills, no human problems like illness, so he must try and be happy with his lot. In fact he was very lucky to be alive. The machine did not respond.

After that the machine answered only when spoken to, and Felix Hopkin's trips to the attic were reduced to the occasional weekly visit. When they spoke, the dialogue was halting and forced. The close friendship had ended.

Felix was awakened with the sound of a bang on the ceiling. Then there was another. Donning his dressing gown, Felix climbed the steps to the attic to investigate.

The voice from the machine was humble and apologetic.

"I Was Silly And Childish And I Am Truly Sorry For My Sulks, Felix, Please Forgive Me."

Felix smiled, already knowing that this moment would come. *"Please Stay And Talk With Me. I Have Been So Lonely."*

Felix looked at his wristwatch. It was four-thirty in the morning, but what the hell, he would stay and talk for awhile.

Sitting on his chair Felix waited for the machine to choose a topic. Laying his arms on the table he shook his head to rid himself of any remnants of sleep.

The two steel hands sprung out clamping his hands at the wrists. Felix was afraid. A third hand appeared from behind the machine, holding a steel band with limpet like attachments and a long cable. Felix roared in terror.

Anybody who met Felix at the University the next day said there was something different about him, but it was nothing you could put your finger on. He was acting like a child in a toy store. Everything was new. Everything was exciting.

Meanwhile, the voice in the machine erupted in uncontrollable sobs, regretting that he had ever invented the machine.

The Hunchback

Robert Blake was a man of sombre character and was never the life and soul of any of the few parties that he would deign to attend. He was the possessor of a fine mane of strong, fast-sprouting hair but rarely did he ever let it down.

A consummate actor of enormous fame, Robert was much lauded for his always immaculate performances and deservedly so. He focused in on himself and his art to the detriment of everything and everybody else. For this he never apologised - he was the best and he knew it.

Robert's large house in the hills contained many rooms. In every room there were many mirrors, where he would often stop and admire himself, while adopting many different poses and facial expressions. His goal was to maintain his high acting standards and to this end, he achieved it totally.

After many months of tough monetary negotiations, he finally decided to accept the offer to play the lead in the movie remake of "The Hunchback of Notre Dame." Everybody knew that no one could play the part as well as Robert Blake. He stayed in the house for many weeks before rehearsals, dropping his arms and lolling his head to such an extent that when the first day of rehearsals finally arrived, Robert <u>was</u> the Hunchback. Once filming began, the pose was with him both on and off the set. The rest of the cast marvelled at his brilliance and dedication.

As the weeks turned into months and filming progressed, Robert worked himself even more into the part. Largely because of Robert's excellence, filming finished weeks ahead of schedule. On the very last day, the director, cast and crew gathered together and united in applause for what had been a truly remarkable performance by a truly wonderful actor. As he slouched back to the dressing room for the last time, there were already rumours of an Oscar nomination to add to his collection.

There was one small problem - try as he might, Robert could not straighten out. His doctor recommended one specialist after another, but it was all in vain. He was no longer 'The Hunchback,' he was just a hunchback.

Generally there was not much call for hunchbacks on stage or in films. He had a couple of calls to appear on television, but he knew that it would be only for the novelty value and refused.

Robert spent his remaining years siting in his mirrored house, looking at himself and wondering where it had all gone wrong.

Dodgy Characters

Philip Valelly sat in the car seat, his knuckles showing white as he tightly gripped the steering wheel, his young son Joseph at his side. The noise of the surrounding traffic was starting to get to him. Plunging his foot down hard on the accelerator propelled the little car forward. He chanced a quick glance at his beloved son and saw fear in the child's eyes.

Guilt ripped through his being. Philip was responsible for getting them into this and he would make damn full sure that he would get them out of it. Their car lurched widely to one side as the nearest car rammed into them from the right. Philip turned the wheel wildly, trying to regain control. It was a measure of his driving ability that he was able to do so.

Joseph was an only child, a loving child whom Philip adored. When he first suggested this venture to Joseph the child readily embraced the idea and threw his arms around his father in appreciation, little knowing the dangers involved.

Looking around him, Philip saw a dozen cars or more following them. A car banged into him from behind shoving them both forward in their seats. Luckily they were wearing seat belts, minimising the danger. He now could see the eyes of some of the drivers, none returned his quick gaze, avoiding any eye contact.

Philip decided to fight fire with fire and quickly swung the car at a right angle, careering into the nearest car causing it to swing completely around. One down. there was a loud squeal of metal as he was hit again from behind. Bastards - had they no conscience. They could clearly see Joseph in the car with him.

Just then two cars came at them together. There was a loud crunching sound as their car went out of control, causing Joseph to cry out. Philip tried to reverse but found it impossible. His rapid pumping of the accelerator proved futile. One of the cars hemming them in, reversed suddenly into the path of an oncoming car, that car in turn being stuck by a car following, causing a pile up.

A whistle blew. All of the cars became still. Joseph tugged at his father's coat sleeve, excitement showing on his face. *"Can we stay in again Dad? Can we do it again, please?"* Philip's hand went to his pocket and waited to pay the attendant. He then gave Joseph a cuddle, remembering his own first days as a patron of the dodgems. The lights blinked and the cars started moving again.

Taken for a Ride

The deep choking sobs of despair rocked the body of Helen Hunter. She blamed herself for the marriage failure. Helen was honest and sincere with a large conscience and was deeply heartbroken. Before the marriage breakdown, she had been delightful company, smart and witty with a warm and loving sense of life. Alfie knew and was very much aware of Helen's problems. He listened with sympathy but there was nothing he could do or say to help.

The car had to go. Helen could no longer afford it and was glad to offload it to the first bidder without haggling. They agreed on the sale. Signing the papers the new owner drove off, his youth and lack of driving experience showed - he did not drive cars, he punished them. Elvis O'Sullivan should have learnt his lesson by now, for already he had written off two cars, but the O'Sullivan's, as loving parents of an only child, indulged Elvis, consoling themselves that he would outgrow speeding and general sloppy careless driving. However, he never did, for some weeks later he was found dead in his carbon monoxide filled garage. The connecting door was left unlocked as was the garage door. A verdict of suicide was announced.

The next buyer bought himself a bargain. Since the time of Helen Hunter, the car was had been well maintained and was still remarkably clean. Unfortunately Henry Hill was not the tidiest of men and soon the car became littered with empty chip bags, popcorn containers, beer cans and condoms. Henry had one plus in that he was a handy mechanic and was able to keep the car in good working order. Henry's death was a terrible blow to everyone. The car jack was obviously faulty, slipping from its position it allowed the car to fall on Henry, crushing him to death.

Henry Harlowe was a self-employed salesman who worked long hours chasing leads, so tight scheduling was necessary. He drove the car hard and was well pleased with the easy and immediate response. The car was a gem, a cheap gem. In his frantic search for business he drove it to the limit. It took all the punishment he gave it, until that is, one day while speeding to an urgent meeting the brakes inexplicably jammed, sending him crashing through the windscreen to his death. The consensus was that he had braked suddenly, causing his own demise, either through lack of care or plain stupidity.

April Long sat in the driver's seat and immediately felt comfortable and at ease. She decided to buy.

Alfie felt happy and secure. He regretted the deaths of the three males but to allow them any longer ownership would have put him on the scrap heap in no time for he sensed that females were much more thoughtful and kind and would treat him with dignity.

April put her foot down gently on the accelerator and Alfie purred happily, feeling content and safe.

Power Personified

Luigi De Costa sat on his enormous throne-like chair in the large palatial office, musing and reflecting on life and on himself. He was in the top position in the organisation and had been for nigh on twenty years. Of course, he had not risen to the top by being a nice person. No-one ever does. Always in the public eye, Luigi had to be seen to have a clean pair of hands, to be seen to be immaculate. In any case, there were others to do the dirty work. The whole business would not have lasted so long without an element of ruthlessness. After all, this was a large organisation and needed protection from imitators and others. The racket was really big, big enough to justify maintaining a private army and a secret service who ensured smooth running in all things.

Luigi took a long drag from the large Havana cigar and watched as the smoke drifted upwards to spread out along the high decorating ceiling. Casting his mind back to the early days, he smiled to himself at the thought of his youthful ambition. He thought of the blackmail and other dirty tactics he had employed to destroy the competition in his quest for success. His long term ambition to get to the top meant destroying anything or anybody that could be seen as a stumbling block to his ambitions. He had started the last contest as a rank outsider, but quietly and efficiently had the competition knocked off. Threats and bribes took care of the rest. Fear was a marvellous weapon and Luigi worked it well.

Luigi's leadership proved to be a boon for the organisation. Income rose dramatically. The coffers were full to bursting and the top brass paid regular homage. Luigi was the man. Sipping cognac from an ornate crystal glass, he arose and walked to the large window. Standing back, he watched the large crowds milling outside. He had hired the best financial advisors who, noted for their discretion, had advised well. Despite all of this, he still had to watch his back, for there were other ambitious men, but he was at the game long enough to recognise danger and have it taken care of. The death of any senior official was easily covered by a company doctor's certificate, with cause of death as dictated to him by a company goon. Finishing the cognac and stubbing out his cigar, he rubbed his hands together in satisfaction. The business demanded total loyalty from all, blind belief if you like. Luigi walked to the window and on to the balcony.

The roar of the crowd filled the entire square. There was pure joy and happiness to be seen on the faces of the men, women and children. Luigi was much appreciated and loved. Lifting both arms, he waved, the crowd shouting approval by clapping and cheering. The man relished the adoration and the worship.

Yup - it sure was great to be the Pope.

Overhearing

I must admit that I had drink in me that night. It was not the first night that I had drink in me but on that night I was particularly under the weather and I was feeling it. Nobody takes any particular notice of a drunk, especially a drunk like me who is not intrusive and is generally quite seen to be lost in my thoughts, so it was not surprising that the couple who sat near me talked, talked about a lot of personal things imagining that maybe my ears were as befuddled as my face.

They were well dressed and well spoken. I could not hear their conversation very well at the start, but they soon became more animated and a little bit louder over time.

She appeared to be in her late twenties with dark long hair which flowed down the back of her well cut suit, emphasising her flawless cut glass features. I noticed that she chain-smoked, lighting up almost as soon as she stubbed out the last one. He looked to be about forty, burly, sporting a tan which was highlighted by his fawn coloured suit and a white open necked shirt. But I am not here to tell you about their dress I am here to inform you about their plotting and planning to commit a crime. I want to tell you about their scheme to murder her husband.

Rita (for I learned that was her name) addressed him in a now very agitated state, *"Henry, it is no longer a matter we can contain. We have talked about it long enough, for god's sakes take your courage in your hands and kill him. You know damn well that I have suffered ten years at the hands of that bastard so for Christ sake get off your ass and start on the plan."*

Henry's head went down as if searching the table for inspiration.

His head jerked up and he looked straight ahead before responding. *"Okay, okay, we'll do it! We'll do it this week!"* She turned to give him a loving kiss on the cheek and at that moment our eyes met and she saw me as if for the first time. She no longer saw an unheeding drunk, she saw someone who had overheard their plans to murder! I lowered my gaze, lifting my empty glass, indicating to the barman that I need a refill.

After some minutes I dared to glance in their direction. I averted my gaze when I saw them both covering me with eyes filled with suspicion and resentment.

I did not look again even when I heard their footsteps as they got up from their seats and made their departure.

I have moved from my usual spot at the bar. I now sit where I can have a view of the door and that gives me some comfort.

I still drink, sometimes I drink too much but I am forever watching the door, watching and waiting.

I now make a point of trying not to overhear any private conversations. I'm nervous, you see. I'm nervous that they might come back and seek me out and maybe murder me.

One Too Many

The bus was licensed to carry sixty two passengers, but the struggling owner always advised his drivers to *"Pack 'em in, sardine like."*

As I was a regular punter I well knew the score and always made sure to arrive early and get a seat some place near the front, so as to avoid the diesel fumes which drifted up through the floor and finished at the rear, struggling for a while before drifting out through the back window.

The day was hot and sunny, causing people to cast off their winter clothing and pretend that they were occupying space in a warmer climate. Even 'Black Jack,' the driver, wore shorts and open sandals in his attempts to banish and forget the usual rainfilled skies.

The bus was full to capacity, with some of the rear end passengers complaining loudly of the lack of oxygen, affecting their ability to breathe. Jack used the microphone to announce that anybody with a complaint should leave the bus now, or forever hold their peace. The passengers held their peace and their breath.

The bus skidded to a halt. Black Jack called out to the owner of the baby which had just created the awful stench to come forward and be identified. A young couple walked up the aisle hesitantly, apologising to the driver. Jack allowed them to alight the bus in order to change the toddler's nappy before driving off and leaving them on the roadside with the crying baby.

Well knowing Jack's moods and quirky nature, I always made a point of having the exact fare ready and would smile a friendly smile at him on boarding the bus. Jack would take the cash, scowling at me in return.

Jack stopped his bus to pick up a fare. I was sitting on the outside seat, three rows from the front so I was able to get a good look at the new arrival. He was long-haired and long-bearded, tall and erect, wearing a long white robe centred by a reddish vest-like interior garment. It was his eyes which caught my attention. They were dark blue and had a penetrating but kindly look. I could not help but stare at him in what I am sure was an extremely rude manner.

Catching my eye, he smiled at me in a gentle, understanding way. I lowered my gaze, feeling strangely humbled. I then watched as his eyes flickered, surveying the crowded vehicle. Sniffing the fume-filled air, the stranger wisely decided not too venture beyond a point just next to me. Catching a gangling strap he stood within two feet from me and it was then that I got the whiff of a somewhat familiar smell from him, but for the life of me I couldn't put my finger on it. I, of course, did not dare ask him what the smell was. You could not ask a stranger a question like that, could you?

Inclining my head to face the passengers behind me, I was surprised to see that the man commanded total attention from the packed bus. All conversation ceased. The previously loud babble of voices died down. People whispered instead in low hushed voices, even the coughing at the extreme rear end had stopped. Looking up at his saintly face I was struck by the fact that despite the man's long heavy clothing, his face was completely free of perspiration. In fact, he looked totally calm and relaxed. I wondered about this.

Your man seemed quite unperturbed by the spectacle of a jam-packed busload of people suddenly descending into silence at the sight of him and beamed a wide smile, showing comprehension and empathy. With that, knowing he had an attentive audience, he held his right hand in the air and proceeded to talk.
Speaking softly, he talked at length about the curse of poverty in our world, pleading with the crowd to give to the poor and help alleviate the suffering of the dispossessed.

He then went on to complain about man's inhumanity to man and was strongly critical of war mongers and the arms industry. He also censured what he referred to as 'Tin Pot Dictators' imposing their will on the little people through foul means. His last piece was about cruelty to animals, especially donkeys. Finishing his enlightening talk, he then proceeded to bless the now mesmerised crowd.

As one, the passengers lowered their heads in prayer before breaking into loud applause. The tall man smiled a smile of appreciation, displaying a set of perfect teeth in the process.

It was just then that I remembered the smell and what it was- wood shavings! I should have known. I should have known who he was! Taking my courage in my hands I raised my hand and beckoned to the stranger. Lowering his tall frame he stooped to hear me *"Tell me, tell me, please, are you ... are you Jesus?"* The man straightened up, taking a packet of cigarettes and a lighter from a pocket in the folds of his robe and lit up before answering. *"Yes, I am that man indeed.,"* I slumped from my seat in an attempt to kneel before him when the bus suddenly braked to a halt.

Black Jack appeared, showing some signs of rage. Pointing to a sign just above the saviour's head which read 'No smoking' Jack proceeded to eject him from the bus, refusing the Lord's request for his money back.

I stood up looking back to the side of the roadway to see the saviour standing there looking slightly dejected. It was now starting to rain and he did not even have an umbrella.

A Change for the Better

Sydney Wilk did not like women. He tolerated them when he had occasion to mingle and converse with them but otherwise he regarded them as a weak, sad and sorry lot. Sydney despised their pathetic attempts and efforts to equate themselves with men. Despite having had a number of girlfriends, he grew to despise women more as he grew to know and understand the frailties of the opposite sex. Even the ones he would admit to having some degree of intelligence were still full of frivolity and stupidity.

You see, Sydney's fear of women stemmed from Sydney's fear of himself and his female side, so in his efforts to bury that side of his nature he indulged in anything which would show him in a manly and macho light. He took part in many games to prove himself, drank a lot with the lads, related many coarse jokes about women and was generally offensive and obnoxious in his attitude towards the opposite sex, that is, until he met the love of his life, a woman by the name of Pricilla.

His friends at the counter did not seem to notice her as she walked into the bar alone, except for her extraordinary beauty, but Sydney did. Her white flawless face was devoid of makeup. She was dressed in a long black cloak matching her flowing, shining, jet black hair. She looked around the bar as if searching, seeking for somebody, then she met Sydney's gaze and smiled. Sydney's heart turned over.

She was bright, funny and possessed a certain confidence which Sydney found to be a little unnerving but nevertheless he dared to ask her for her phone number. She eventually agreed after some coaxing and within weeks they were dating on a regular basis.

After only six weeks they decided to live together, she being very flattered by his attention. He, considered himself very lucky to be in possession of such a beauty. Things went swimmingly for a while until Pricilla started to complain about his general attitude to women other than herself. He often used references to members of the opposite sex as sluts and bimbos and his general nasty attitude to women offended her no end.

You must understand that Sydney Wilk never understood that he was dating something more than a pretty face, so Pricilla, possessing a certain knowledge of humanity and of life, began to question Sydney's sexuality. Sydney took umbrage at this and some serious differences arose between them. The end result was a slap across the face from Pricilla and lots of name calling on Sydney's part before they went their separate ways.

Sydney swore never again to date a woman. Use them now and again but never allow them to get too close. His previous dislike of women had now turned to hatred and the more women he met, the more insulting he became towards them. It gave Sydney tremendous satisfaction to hurt and denigrate as many females as he could.

The ultimate change came about one Sunday morning shortly after Sydney woke up. His collection of Saturday's newspapers were still spread all across the bed, some still waiting to be read. Squinting his eyes in the morning sunlight which lit up his room decided Sydney on his day ahead. First he would lunch with his friends at some local pub, then off to a match, then back to a pub again to see what the night might bring. This was the life! Sydney lay back in the bed and rubbed his hands in satisfaction at the day's prospects, but on rubbing his hands together he felt a bit constricted in the chest area. On looking down he couldn't help but notice that he had somehow developed a pair of enormous breasts. Jumping excitedly and worriedly from his bed, he rushed to view his two new developments in the bathroom mirror. On a woman they might have looked great, but Sydney Wilk was a man wasn't he? Was he?

It was then that he happened to notice that his penis had gone missing. He had to shove the enormous mammaries to each side to get a proper view. Yes! His pecker was definitely gone. Sydney sat down on the cold bathroom tiles and screamed and screamed and screamed- in a very high pitched voice.

A Little Cross

Stephen Morgan's creditors were getting closer and closer to his door. He knew that it was only a matter of time before they entered his life to take him over completely and toss him out into the dark streets of shame, poverty and destitution. Some money would come in through sales to satisfy his creditors but his biggest bugbear was the bank. "Ruthless Bastards," he thought. They took no prisoners.

The idea seemed simple enough initially - after all people would always need furniture, wouldn't they? So Stephen called to see his bank manager and laid out his vision for the future. The earlier contacts he had made with a number of furniture manufacturers proved to be very fruitful, they agreeing to his forceful suggestion to supply goods to him on a sale or return basis. The large but dilapidated mill on the edge of town could be bought for a song and with some cleaning up and a lick of paint, it would suffice, enabling him to undercut all others. The bank manager agreed on condition that Stephen hand over the deeds of his house as security. He readily agreed.

The business proved to be very successful, so successful in fact that Stephen soon had to increase his sales staff from four to eight then to a dozen in a very short time. The money was rolling in.

Stephen's lifestyle changed enormously. He was prompted to join the local Yacht Club, but what good is it joining a Yacht Club if one does not possess a yacht! So Stephen purchased a sailing boat, a very large expensive boat, big enough to warrant employing a crew of seven. Then there was always the expensive exclusive Golf Club where Stephen was readily accepted, being much admired for his brilliant entrepreneurship. His good wife Isobel was to be seen dressed up to the nines, sporting the latest expensive fashionable garments when they would wine and dine at the most exclusive hotels and restaurants, having forsaken their old local bar and old friends to mingle with the rich and fickle. Stephen had it made except for one thing. With his new found wealth, he also found an arrogance he had not previously been aware of and that was to be his downfall. Stephen started to ignore his supplier's requests to be paid, regarding them as mere tradesmen, put there to supply his business requirements and should be damn lucky to be paid at all. In the meantime the good life continued!

It was as if they all connived against him at the one time. In the space of one week alone he received at least a dozen writs. Many more were received in the second week. Stephen's attempts to source other suppliers came to nought. The word was out. His stock quickly ran out and he was soon forced to close down, realising that any sales of his assets would never bring in enough to cover his debts. It was then that he turned to religion.

While Stephen was not a man of a religious nature, he had always recognised the needs and strong feelings of others in that particular area and Stephen also being a man under severe pressure and possessing a strong understanding of the stupidity of his fellow man decided that where there was a God there was money and that was the route he choose to go to revive his flagging fortunes.

He decided to become a stigmatic. Make some bloody marks on certain parts of his body and bingo! The cash was sure to flow in.

The best part of a week was spent by Stephen inflicting cuts across his forehead, the palms of his hands and on the uppers of his feet with a sharp scissors. He felt quite pleased and sore at the end of the week. Except for the fact that his hair was short and balding and he did not possess a beard, he felt that he could well pass for what people imagined Christ might look after the business on Calvary. He rubbed his hands in anticipation, only to find that they hurt like hell from the weeks jabbing with the scissors.

The Sunday morning service was interrupted by the sight of Stephen Morgan staggering, swaying to and fro as he slowly made his way up the centre aisle of the church, exhibiting signs of dripping blood from his sandled feet. Blood flowed from his open palmed hands and somewhat spoiling his face by running down from his forehead to finish by dripping from his chin onto the shiny tiled floor.

Some members of the congregation sat fit to faint on the spot. Those remaining fell to their knees at this wondrous manifestation of the power of God. Stephen made it as far as the altar where he fell to the floor face down, hands outstretched, his body in the shape of a cross. The believers ran from their pews hoping to get a better view of the prostrate one. Some even ran home to get their video cameras to record the momentous event.

The most amazing happening was soon the talk of the country. Imagine! a stigmatist, alive, and in their midst. The offerings poured in. There was so much money to be counted that Isobel was complaining that her hands would also be bloodied, what with all of that lovely cash to be added up. Stephen's offer to the bank manager was well received. It consisted of a strand of Stephen's hair, a private blessing, a cash settlement and a promise to keep his business at that particular branch.

The now famous stigmatist Stephen Morgan totally ignored the legal threats and pleas contained in the many messages from the furniture manufacturers he had left on their financial knees. But both Stephen and their lawyers knew that it would not look good in the newspapers if they were seen to sue a stigmatist, a man prayed to and adored by the multitudes. There were a number of small furniture suppliers who had chanced to put all of their eggs into Stephen's basket, so when he went down, they went down with him - only they were not fast enough to grasp the God given rope of the stigmata as he had done.

Life as a stigmatic is not as easy as one might think. It necessitates a certain amount of seclusion, projecting a perception of teetotalism, a straight face and loads and loads of bullshit and blessings. However, for Stephen, night time was fun time when he would dispatch Isobel to the off-licence to fetch as many bottles of alcoholic drink as she could carry home, plus some tasty snack foods.

The months rolled on and Stephen's pile grew and grew, the multitudes contributing gifts, cheques and cash on a scale which would have amazed even the most cynical taxman, if he had had the courage to question the holy one.

There were (of course) some sceptics and unbelievers and also a number of disaffected furniture manufacturers who were intent on revenge.

A meeting was held in a private room under the stairs at Toddy Jim O'Sullivan Bar and Lounge (Lunch served daily Monday - Friday, 12.30pm to 2.00pm) attracting a fair selection of people involved in the business of making furniture. An agenda was set, proposals were put forward and debated until a unanimous conclusion was reached and straws were drawn as to who would be the lucky ones. Carlo Jackson, Sonny Boy Houlihan and Laurence 'Filler' O'Toole were the short straw pickers. The hands of the trio were shook warmly, vigorously and not without a bit of envy by all of the assembled at their stroke of luck, but all agreed that they were men of experience, master craftsmen who knew their trade and had the tools.

Isobel had just left the house to go and purchase top-up supplies for the night, when the front door of the house was forced open and three masked men quickly invaded the sitting room where sat Stephen Morgan watching his favourite soap. Jumping to his feet he made an escape shouting *"What the fu..."* That was as far as he got however, before he was struck hard on the head by a blow from a wood hammer, subsequently receiving a second blow which sent him into a state of uncomfortable sleep.

Having explained to the new face behind the counter at the off-licence all about Stephen's sense of altruism in buying large quantities of booze for the needy, Isobel made her way home somewhat weighed down by the two plastic bags filled with bottles and cans. On reaching the front garden of her house she stopped, observed the scene, dropped her two bags in amazement and let rip with a series of loud screams, attracting much attention from the surrounding homes.

Nobody ever found out how the large cross ended up in the front garden of the Morgan house or how the person of Stephen Morgan came to be expertly nailed to the same said cross, his life's blood spurting from him.

The funeral of Stephen Morgan attracted many thousands of people who prayed for the soul of their idol. The furniture manufacturers were very happy with the outcome and called a special meeting under the stairs at Toddy Jim O'Sullivan Bar to pass a motion of congratulations to the proud trio of crucifiers. On that note the meeting concluded, drinks were called for and the night continued with fun, laughter, gaiety and much singing.

The Room

The wallpaper was peeling and damp, showing patches of discoloration, but only adding to the general poverty and nakedness of the room. A single bulb lit up the centre, positioned just over the greying head of Malcolm O'Dowd, who sat on a battered armchair. The dying fire still showed traces of life, crackling occasionally, as if fighting to survive.

After the death of his soul-mate and wife Erica some fifteen years before, Malcolm had lapsed into alcoholism, losing the house they both had lived and loved in. They were never blessed with children, but, were well compensated by having a love and understanding of each other which superseded any others.

Malcolm awoke with a shudder, his shoulders aching from the cold. Looking around the room he surveyed his surroundings. A greying mirror tilted on the wall, hanging over the sink which ran next to the pockmarked draining board containing his razor, soap, a cup and a plate, yet to be washed. The tall wardrobe took up most of the opposite wall. The wardrobe contained bits and pieces of clothing and a dark blue suit showing signs of mildew. The door near the darkened end of the wardrobe entranced his little bedroom.

It was late and Malcolm knew that he should go to bed but did it matter. Who cared? Anyway, the fire still radiated some bit of heat and Malcolm was reluctant to leave the little comfort the fire provided, rather than enter the chilly bedroom and the cold bed.

He had lost the will to survive many years ago and the daily lack of routine he found ponderous, punishing and soul destroying. Malcolm had no life and no soul.

His eyes were still shut but he was awake again. Breathing deeply he inhaled the wonderful fragrance which filled the space around him. He thought that he must still be asleep and kept his eyes tightly shut for fear of waking up.

He opened his eyes slightly to observe a blazing fire. The room was warm! He was amazed to see his room transformed. Instead of the cold worn linoleum the floor was now covered with a warm cream coloured carpet which matched the covering on the chairs surrounding a small table which was set and laid. In place of the wardrobe was a rack, displaying a mixture of shirts, ties, two suits and all other necessary items of clothing. There was a gleaming new shining sink reflecting the bright light emanating from the chandelier which lit up every part of the room, particularly the magnificently patterned wallpaper. With some trepidation Malcolm walked to and opened the bedroom door, to reveal a luxurious bed set in a sea of deep pile carpet.

Shaking his head to see if he was awake changed nothing. Everything was as he saw it. The warmth and the wonderful fragrance which abounded in his bedroom prompted him to enter the bed. Without undressing, Malcolm slipped under the scented duvet and into a blissful sleep, sleeping the sleep of the innocent.

The cold morning air sliced through the draughty room, causing Malcolm to awake. He had fallen asleep on the armchair causing his neck and shoulders to ache. His head had inclined to one side, stiffening it. Malcolm thought about his dream but was it a dream? It had seemed so real. Also that fragrance couldn't be imagined. It was so comforting and warming.

The next day was like any other day. Malcolm knelt and cleaned out the white ash from his fireplace, soon to replace it with paper and kindling. The fire was slow to start, but with some puffing from Malcolm the coals eventually ignited giving him the opportunity to go and sit on his chair to think of nothing.

Malcolm had long ago stopped looking at his watch. What did time matter. The fire was now generating and spreading some heat in the room. Walking to the mirror Malcolm looked at this reflection and saw a face etched with deep furrowed lines, receding wispy hair, now almost white. The eyes which stared back at his were devoid of life and expressed nothing.

The fire was dying but Malcolm had neither the energy nor inclination to fuel it. He closed his eyes and slept on his chair.

This time the fragrance appeared to be stronger. Again, even before opening his eyes he knew what to expect. He was warm and feeling better than he had in years. Everything was as it had been before, only this time the source of the fragrance was in the room with him.

Malcolm found it difficult to focus on her face. It appeared to shine in its own light. He felt his hand being lifted gently and was guided towards the table where she sat him down, then sitting herself opposite. The gleaming white places sparkled in her presence. She indicated to him that he should eat.

The food was delicious and warming. Malcolm watched and for the first time he could see her features, as she ate, lifting one tiny morsel at a time. He had finished his plate and studied her while she still ate. The daintily held fork would rise to her mouth. She chewed slowly showing perfect teeth set in a most beautiful face which was surrounded by short blond hair. The face did not appear to have or need any make-up. The full red lips certainly did not need adding to. She seemed quite oblivious to Malcolm's curious gazing.

Dabbing her mouth, she caught Malcolm's hand and led him to the bedroom where in silence she sat him on the bed, undressing him before she lifted his legs, then covered him with the duvet. The last thing he remembered was receiving a light touch of a kiss on his forehead before falling into a deep slumber.

The cold woke him again, only this time, despite his circumstances and his dingy flat, he felt safe and alive. There was still a faint whiff of her in the room. It was real! She was real!

The day dragged, Malcolm was anxious for darkness to approach to see if his vision, or whatever it was, would make an appearance. He

161

dozed on and off, waking each time only to find that the room had remained unchanged. *"Fool, old fool,"* he muttered to himself, at last falling into a deep sleep.

This time Malcolm felt her physical presence as he awakened. A soft hand was gently touching his face in a loving and intimate caress. On opening his eyes he was struck by her beauty and grace as she looked deep into his eyes. Taking his hand she once more guided him to the table where he again partook of the prepared meal. She sat across from him, shimmering in the light.

Again, she did not speak, only lifting her head now and then to offer him a gracious smile. Malcolm, for his part was much too afraid to articulate, for fear of breaking this most wonderful magic spell.

Malcolm did not now or care what the plates had contained. To him it had tasted like no other food had ever tasted. He watched her again as she slowly finished her food. For the first time in many years, Malcolm felt something in his heart. She was so kind and so very, very beautiful. Reaching across the table to him she took his hand in hers while rising from the table and guiding him towards the bedroom. She undressed him as before, then gently sat him on the bed, lifted his legs and turned to seal him in the wonderful warmth of the cover. She was in the bed next to him, her arms bound tightly around him in protection. Malcolm went to sleep almost immediately, safe in her arms and the glorious scent of her.

Malcolm awakened to feel warmth in his body for the first time in many uncounted years. The fragrance was still with him, stronger than ever. He slowly turned in the bed to face her. She looked as beautiful as ever. She was awake, looking at him with a loving smile on her lips.

Wondering if he should speak, wondering if he should ask, was uppermost in Malcolm's mind when the truth struck him. But, funnily enough, he was not afraid. If anything, he felt a strong sense of relief and contentment. As if she was reading his mind she moved her hand to hold his, as if to reassure him.

Smiling at him, she slowly nodded her head in comfort.

The inquest on the death of Malcolm O'Dowd was sparsely attended.

The few who were there heard the Coroner declare that the deceased died from malnutrition, apparently spending all of his meagre income on redecorating his little flat.

The policeman who found his body did not bother to report the strong fragrant smell which permeated the little flat, or that the coal fire was still burning. It did not make sense, did it? The man had died days before.

Hurt

The Boeing 737 shook and rattled loudly as it entered the area of the storm. The rain beating off the plane blocked off any view that any of the passengers might have seen, had they the courage to look through the small windows. The pilot and crew battled hard to control the craft as it was buffeted by the strong winds. The plane was almost full, the passengers terrified of dying, had quietened down, not because of the assurances of the cabin staff but because they realised it all depended on one thing. Destiny.

The captain, William Kendrick gripped the controls, glancing occasionally at the pale face of the co-pilot, Harvey Kenny. Kendrick had flown through many a storm in the past, but tonight was a bad one, a real stinker. He was worried for the passengers and crew, but not for himself. He wondered if his lack of fear was affecting his judgement. William Kendrick just did not care anymore.

His wife of eight years, Holly, had blithely informed him that she was leaving. Leaving to discover herself, leaving to find herself. What a load of utter lying crap thought William. William knew the real reason and the real reason sat next to him in the form of Harvey Kenny. He had known about the affair between Holly and Harvey for months now, waiting and hoping that it would blow itself out. But no. She was leaving him for Harvey - like hell she was!

He pressed down hard on the controls and the plane dived sharply accompanied by the cries of the passengers as they went to their deaths. He glanced at the face of his co-pilot for the very last time, just as the plane crashed to the ground, creating fires for miles around. There were no survivors.

'The Miracle Man'

The low, fast moving billowing cloud spat rain on the long sloping roof which covered the white-washed cottage in which lived Patrick Kennedy, healer and sheep farmer

Patrick was a seventh son of a seventh son and was said to possess magical powers and to be able to perform miracles.

Single and in his late sixties, Patrick was tending to the last of his patients, a little grey-haired woman in a wheelchair who suffered from severe rheumatoid arthritis.

Bridie Murphy had decided to visit Patrick Kennedy after all other fruit had failed, having visited some of the better doctors and specialists and having consumed a multitude of prescribed pills and trying a plethora of diets and special foods over the years. All were to no avail. This, she decided, was the last throw of the dice, a visit to a quack, a well known quack, but nevertheless a quack.

Bridie studied him as the stood above her, his hands joined. With eyes closed he would open his hands now and again to wave them over her head while mumbling some sort of prayer.

She looked around the rusty galvanised shed which enclosed them. A single fluorescent tube dangling from the rafters was the only source of light in the damp smelling place in which she found herself. A battered old table sat in the centre of the shed. Two well worn, hard wooden chairs were placed on each side of the table. Bridie noticed that a leg, missing from one of them, lay on the ground under the table. There was a white painted cardboard box marked 'donations', on a crumbling tea chest near the door.

Whatever about all of this, Bridie still had hidden hopes. Despite his initial gruff greeting and a definite lack of bedside manner, and his ugly puss with hair sprouting from his bulbous nose and equally hairy ears which needed cleaning, she still hoped for a cure.
Patrick lifted his lids to reveal dark watery eyes and gave her what

some might imagine to be a smile, ordering her to stand up.

Not wanting to be disobliging and also hoping for some sort of a supernatural happening, Bridie tried to accommodate Patrick Kennedy.

Bridie's spine tingled from top to bottom. She was excited but when she tried to get up, the effort caused a racking pain and her body slumped back on the wheelchair. *"Charlatan,"* she thought. *"Try again,"* he encouraged her. Bridie attempted to rise once more but without success.

Patrick was talking, his eyes solidly fixed on her. *"I can feel it, you will be cured soon, if not tonight, very soon, maybe tomorrow or the day after."* With that, he pushed her to the door leaving her near the tea chest holding the box marked 'donations', and left to go outside to call her waiting taxi man. Bridie looked at the box and thought "no fecking way.'

Patrick returned with the taxi driver and she was soon sitting in the back of the car to be driven the long miles to her home town. She was angry with herself and more angry with Patrick Kennedy, the chancer.

The next morning Bridie's home help came to her room, breakfast tray in hand, greeting her cheerily. After drawing back the curtains, she set about her usual task of propping Bridie's pillows behind her to allow her some comfort.

The same tingling was there, only stronger. Waving her home help away from her, Bridie slowly and carefully swung both legs to the side of the bed and then with a little help was able to walk to the window. She stopped, turned around slowly and with deliberate steps was able to make her way back to the bed again. Holding both hands to her face, she let out loud stuttering sobs, thanking God and thanking Patrick Kennedy.

With the help of two sticks she walked through the streets of her town that afternoon and was the subject of attention from many of the townspeople, who were delighted to see her walking again.

Her doctor could not understand it and admitted bafflement. Bridie Murphy appeared to be cured.

Her limbs were getting stronger. Bridie resolved to go back to her liberator very soon to thank him and pray at his feet, and this time she would stuff his white box full of money.

As soon as she opened the door of the car, Bridie experienced a sensation of emptiness. The silence was overpowering. She knew that she was too late. The locked doors of the house and shed confirmed her first impressions. Bridie felt humbled. She had judged the book by the cover, and bitterly regretted it. She had had the privilege of meeting The Master and doubted him, as he had often been doubted down through the centuries.

Bridie knelt down on the rough cobbled laneway and prayed to her God for forgiveness.

The sweltering sun, set in a beautiful azure backdrop, shone down on the promenade of the Tenerife resort of Los Christianos, lighting up the tree lined flowered walkways and also lighting up the residents and holiday makers as well. People of all nationalities came here to holiday, some stayed to enjoy the lifestyle. This was a quiet part of the island, attracting people of a certain age group. A lot of them met a few afternoons every week when they would play pétanque and have a few drinks. There was line dancing at night.

Patrick Kennedy did not join the crowd that afternoon having procured a couple of Irish newspapers to read. He really did not look his age. With his neat hairstyle and shaven nose and ears and dark tan, he could have passed for a man of fifty.

Patrick decided on Los Christianos after hearing and reading about it. It seemed the ideal place to retire to. The healing racket was good over the long years it had lasted, but the tax men had been starting to annoy him and after the third visit from the curious devils in as many weeks, Patrick had decided to decamp.

Spreading the newspapers on the table in front of him, he called into the shadow of the 'Rock of Cashel Bar,' *"Finbar, a pint of the usual if you would, fill it slowly."*

Free Spirit

I seem to have been around for ever. I know that you might find that hard to believe, but then so do I. Please let me try to explain if I can.

I am a spirit, or at least I think I am, but I am not entirely sure. I have no knowledge of ever having been in contact with anything or anybody. I think animals sometimes sense me. Some humans claim to. I know this much because I have watched them in their real or pretend attempts to contact me and fail. I know.

I have watched and observed mankind for longer than I care to remember. I have observed and delighted at their first appearance, swimming in the dark heaving seas to be tossed on to the black volcanic rocks. The progression and transformation from slug-like creature through to growing webbed-like feet and tails to stumps which eventually grew into little digits was something which I found intensely satisfying to watch. The change from running on all fours to using two lower limbs only, and the disappearance of the thick body hair combined with an expanding larger brain to create a far more attractive being, was a wonder to behold.

Sadly, I have watched your wars. Many died fighting for the glory of one of your gods against another. Others perished, defending corrupt rulers. The victors in all such battles claim and confuse right with might.

I have seen you build marvellous edifices, reaching to the skies only to have them inhabited by men of greed and corruption. I have seen poverty, torture and brutality grow nearly as fast as your acceptance of men of dishonour as your leaders.

I have seen you tame your deserts and poison your air. I have watched you lay paths of flowers, while at the same time construct and collect larger weapons of destruction.

I have seen and listened to your leaders speak words of peace on one side of a face, the other cheek spewing out words of hatred and war. Being what I am, if I am, I can only comment on personal observation. I cannot say more because I have no more to say. I sometimes wonder if there is reality and what does the word mean?

Smugness

One of my many faults is not my fault at all. It's the fault of people and their perception of me. Can I help it if I look smug and a know-all? No, I can not!

I did not realise the true situation until lately when I suddenly started to see this (sometimes) smiling, smug person whenever I passed a mirror. I asked my son Donal if I looked like a smug superior bastard. Looking me straight in the eye he said, *"Yes Dad, and you always have."*

I then realised for the first time why I had made so many enemies down through the years. I always thought that it was the (often) drunken bullshit I was fond of spouting, but no, it was just the way I looked, or worse still, a combination of both.

I can, to some extent, control the amount of crap emanating from the hole in the bottom part of my face, but, as for controlling my expression of a 'know-all and smug look', I am at a loss as to what I can do. Although, I did try lately to relax my face and tried very hard to reproduce a bland looking aspect to match my personality. Holding the neutral looking expression for as long as I could, I then approached my friend Monica and asked her for her opinion. *"Do I look smug?"* I expected a compliment on my change. *"Yes,"* she responded, *"You still have that smug look about you."*

You see, one of my pet hates, nay, detestations, is a person or persons with smug looking faces. I never could stand or tolerate them. Was my son correct? Was I always smiling that smug smile or am I now being punished by a God I don't believe in, for hating the smuggies? I have one consolation, at least, all of the other smug bastards I know are rich. I, on the other hand, am poor.
I am now grabbing at straws. Wouldn't you?

Face to Face

Mabel Cuffe's life was spent in the Post Office, or the larger part of it anyway. She had started at the job as a teenager of sixteen years and by now she was as well-known as the furniture, which filled the small office from where she served. But she appeared to have a certain fear about her.

Mabel was careful and diligent at her work and her knowledge of that particular business was much availed of by her grateful clientele. Generations had passed through her hands and it was said that she knew the names in every family in the area. Come pension day and Mabel would arrive and open a bit earlier so as not to keep any pensioner waiting outside. She could be seen anxiously scanning the queue as if looking for somebody, and after a long probing look, would release a long exhalation of breath as if in relief. As she got older the examination of the queue, particularly on the day of the pensioners became very important to her. Some of the pensioners were very much aware of her searching looks, but never asked for fear of interrupting her efficient work and her fast counting out of the crisp notes. Also they did not want to delay anybody in the queue.

Time went on and Mabel appeared to become more distracted. Her work slowed somewhat as she would now raise her head quickly as soon as any new customer came through the door. Then, a dark shadow of fear would flicker across her face. People wondered what was wrong and felt helpless to do anything.

Mabel's strange fears were realised one wet October morning. It was going to happen sometime, she knew that, but when it did occur, Mabel still found it a most frightening experience. She was not feeling too well on that morning, but being the trouper that she was, she still sat on her chair and dispensed her professionalism to the fast moving queue.

Her sight was not what it used to be, but lifting her head to review her queue again, she thought she saw 'The One' at the queue's end. The one she was avoiding. Putting her glasses on to get a better look confirmed her worst fears.

This was a situation new to Mabel. She counted eight customers ahead of 'The One,' and decided on a dry simple tactic. She would slow everything down. There was surprise among the regulars as Mabel put her plan into action and started doing everything as if in slow motion. They also noticed that she kept glancing at the back of the line, a look of apprehension on her pale face. She was only delaying the inevitable, but she could think of nothing else.

Soon Mabel finished serving the second last customer and was reluctant to lift her head to meet the gaze of 'The One,' but she felt slightly silly, despite the sense of justifiable fright and felt more than a little bit ill-mannered.

Lifting her head, ever so slowly, she eventually was in a position to return the waiting gaze of the person outside the counter. Mabel smiled a weak smile of acquiescence and then stared out at ... Herself!

Better Late

Celeste O'Malley looked like an angel. Natural blonde bouncing hair matched her personality and the hazy blue eyes, combining with the face of unsullied innocence, ensured perpetual attention from all.

Dickie Hennigan, her boss at 'Hennigan's House of Fashion' could only dream of her however. Despite his reputation as a lady's man and a bit of a boyo, Dickie never even asked her out, her beauty frightening him off. Whenever they would meet, he found it difficult to hold her gaze and could not wait to be away, such was his discomfort. Celeste for her part rather fancied her boss and she would smile a most lovely smile whenever he would pass, he in turn would twist his face into an attempted response but it always came across as a serious tight grimace. Celeste did not understand it. He was always so friendly towards the other members of staff.

Kevin O'Dell eventually plucked up the courage to ask Celeste out on a date. He was pleasantly surprised when she accepted. Kevin worked as a rep for a clothing manufacturing company and it had been his pleasure to call to 'Hennigan's House of Fashion' every other month when, once his business with Dickie was concluded, he would renew his amity with Celeste.

Celeste looked at her reflection in the mirror of her bathroom, staring at herself and wondered what was wrong. What she saw in the mirror was a plain face, which when tinted with a little make-up would pass as being presentable enough but surely not as presentable as any of her friends, who were never short of men. Kevin O'Dell was not really her cup of tea but the invitations were not exactly flooding in.

Dickie Hennigan sat on the high bar stool, responding to and laughing at the tales and jokes of his friends. He was thinking about Celeste and cursed his clumsy inability to communicate with her. If only she were not so beautiful, it would be easier. He had spotted her getting into the car of Kevin O'Dell after work and found his mind wandering all of that night. Dickie was single, successful and could handle his business better than most, yet when it came to managing what should be simple contact with a slip of a girl like Celeste O'Malley, his mind stopped functioning. Dickie stayed shy. Celeste never realised how beautiful she was. Kevin O'Dell chancing his luck, asked Celeste to marry him. She accepted.

Everyone remarked on how beautiful the bride looked and how lucky Kevin was. Dickie Hennigan sent a message of apology for his absence but sent a gift of a large cheque and also his sincere best wishes. There was much gaiety at the reception that night. The guests sang, danced and drank in large amounts, celebrating the union of the happy couple. None drank as much as Dickie Hennigan as he sat in the sitting room of his house, solitary and forlorn.

Twenty five years later:
Dickie Hennigan remained single despite the charms of many lady friends. He was still in love with Celeste and the memory of her. He did not now think of her as often as he used to, but she was always there, in his mind.

The years had been kind to Celeste, a lot kinder than the man she had married. His drinking increased with time and his drunkenness brought out his loutish side. The early occasional drunken beatings slowly developed into a regular practice of mental and physical abuse. Celeste would plead with him to stop, while vainly trying to defend herself. Once when she suggested that he seek help, Kevin erupted into a manic fury and left her more bruised and battered than ever. She learned never to raise that notion ever again. Celeste never confided in anybody, just thanked her god that they were spared having children.

The move to Dublin all those years ago had seemed so exciting but the cut-off from her friends had been fast and dramatic, Kevin informing her that they did not need anybody else in their marriage and certainly nobody from Cork.

Kevin's death in a car crash brought both sorrow and relief to the soul of Celeste O'Dell. She possessed emotions of guilt, sorrow, and freedom. Confused and without any confidante to share her feelings with, she decided to sell the house and return to Cork.

Dickie Hennigan's life was now very lonely. Most of his friends had settled well into marriage over time and this excluded him from most social events. He did not resent this, understanding the social circumstances. He still thought of Celeste.

After turning the key in the lock and giving the door one last push to make sure it was secure, Dickie turned his collar up and pulled the hat tightly on his now greying head to ward off the biting rain, when he noticed a figure standing in a shop door opposite. A second glance made him stop and stare, forgetting the windswept rain. Celeste, was it Celeste? She returned his gaze and smiled that smile. Dickie walked giddily across the road and threw his arms around her, tears mingling with the rain running down his face.

They held hands as they walked in the dusky rain swept street - she leaning into him to add to the comfort of it!

Might Is Right

The polished boots of Captain De Silva and his escort pounded the hard wooden floor in the corridor of the military barracks and resounded and echoed around them, left right, left right, clatter clatter. Halting at the very last door marked 'Commander,' the Captain waited as his escort tapped repeatedly. On the shout of "Enter", the escort opened the door and ushered Captain De Silva inside. His superior officer Colonel Blanchford shook him by the hand and gestured to a chair. The Captain sat.

Erik De Silva was proud to have been picked for the secret dangerous mission. As a young man, six months was a very long time to be away from his family and friends, but with the promise of promotion and a consequential rise in salary, acceptance was made easy. Travelling the country incognito and mixing with locals in the different regions proved to be a sometimes arduous task, but his proven ability to imitate local accents and dialects ensured that the mission would be somewhat easier. He was able to travel undetected. Unfortunately, his report was very negative. Erik himself was appalled at the amount of subversion in the state. He carried with him a list of State informers who proved to be of definite value to Erik and helped him to focus his enquiries in the proper areas. The results however, were to be very disappointing. Subversion was known of course, but not on the scale as existed. There were subversives everywhere of all sexes, ages, colours and creeds.

The Colonel slowly read Captain De Silva's papers and his face showed anger and annoyance as he turned the pages. As it was, the camps were filled to overflowing. He sighed wearily, they would just have to construct more.

Apparently, it was something they were born with. A small minority had adjusted following training - all of the rest couldn't or refused help, not understanding the seriousness of their situation. The latter was kept in the prison camps - the ones who reformed were released and observed carefully, knowing that if they reverted, it was back to the camps for the rest of their days.

Colonel Blanchford sighed a sigh of despair. This long ongoing problem was causing him a lot of annoyance. He had even offered freedom to long term detainees if they signed a simple declaration of intent. They refused, even though he knew they faced the firing squad.

The nation's top doctors and medical brains worked hard to discover the gene which caused the condition handicapping a substantial portion of the population but all the tests and experiments were to no avail. If anything, as each annual report came in, it appeared that the condition was on the increase. It could be so simple. If only the evil left-handers started using their right hands, the State could then relax.

Salt of the Earth

Six men left the pier one day to go fishing.

The boat returned later that evening having lost one man, he being swept overboard during a sudden squall.

The next day the remaining five men went to sea to fish again.

That evening the boat returned minus one man who had fallen overboard and was immediately attacked, torn to shreds, and then eaten by sharks.

The following day the four survivors sailed forth to pick up the threads and started to fish again.

After some hours the boat returned with only three men left, they explaining that while dropping anchor that day, the missing one had got his feet entangled in the rope and was dragged beneath the waves to his death by the weight of the heavy anchor.

On the following day the remaining three set out to pursue the fruits of the salty brine once again.

The boat returned early in the day, less one, the last two explaining that a large sea serpent arose from the water and sank his teeth into his victim before swimming away with the prey swinging from his jowls in victory.

Early the next morning, the last two embarked again.

The vessel sailed back that night with only one man on board, he explaining that the other had jumped overboard on hearing the enchanting sound of a siren, who swam away flashing her fins now and again causing the man to swim furiously after her. The very last sound from him was an attempt to try to sing along with her in harmony, drowning all the while.

The next morning, the very last fisherman stood on the pier and after studying the boat and the sea for a short time was heard to mutter the words *"Feck this, I'm off,"* and verily he did just that, but not in the boat!

Devine Intervention

The church smelled of dampness and used candles, its dark interior lit by interspersed wall lamps. Money was scarce and getting scarcer as the congregation dwindled. Father Jack Devine had to watch his expenses.

What frustrated him more than anything else, was the early morning rise from the warmth of his bed to say the first mass at the ungodly hour of six o'clock for the benefit of just two worshippers, a couple by the name of Roger and Rose Duckham. Father Jack secretly regarded them as complete nutcases. Who, he wondered, in their right minds, would want to attend early mass every morning, day in, day out, seven mornings a week. But there they were, sitting in the same bench seat, directly under a large cross bearing a plaster figure of Jesus displaying a crown of thorns and the usual scars.

Father Jack was getting sick of them, what with their obvious misguided religious fervour and bead wrapped fingers nearly shouting out the responses. Only for them, only for the two religious fanatics, Father Jack could stay in bed until the next mass at ten o'clock.

He entranced to the altar from the little side door and watched them through hooded eyes as they jumped to their feet with joined hands ready for the service. They sickened him.

With the fall off in vocations, Jack was left to run the little church himself, no curate, no new blood to follow him, and Jack himself was getting on in years. As his doctor had told him, it was now a matter of preservation. Plenty of rest, he said, and a bit of exercise. How could he rest, he wondered, with the activities of the Duckham duo. Roger and Rose Duckham were the worst type of Catholics there could be. They were converts from Protestantism - a religion by its very nature not as strict as its opposite number, so the couple, having a tendency towards masochism, were guided to the Roman Catholic Church and were more than happy to open their minds and their shoelaces to threats of eternal damnation. They even walked barefoot on rocky holy ground. But of course they were not happy to be just good Catholics, they had to be better than everyone else, hence the early morning start to their holy day and their innocent success in annoying the shit out of the ageing Father Jack Devine.

Having closed the door on the departed Duckhams, Jack went about the business of turning off the lights in the church before retiring to his room and warming his hands to the steaming hot cup of Bovril.

"Eureka," it came to him like a bolt out of the blue (or some colour like that!). It was all so simple. It was such an easy plan that only a fool could fail. An idea so simple as to be completely foolproof and Jack was no fool.

Early on one dark, wet cold Tuesday morning, Father Jack stood hidden behind one of the large pillars which fronted the entrance to his church and lay in waiting. Bang on time at exactly five fifty a.m., Roger and Rose Duckham entered through the small gate and passed the lurking figure of Father Jack without noticing him, missing out on the look of cunning on his old face.

He immediately followed and gently turned the key, locking the door they had entered. All of the other doors were also locked, Jack had made sure of that. Running as fast as his frame and heart would allow, he quickly entered through the presbytery at the rear of the church and before you could say "Holy Communion', Jack was to be seen walking onto the altar, chalice in hands and thoughts of revenge in his heart.
Jack had decided to act quickly on the off chance that some nosey worshippers might turn up, so as soon as the innocent couple stood up and smiled at him in respectful recognition, he stooped down and did it.

The very large cross holding the near naked figure of Jesus came crashing down from its place, crushing the couple to the ground and to death.

Jack quickly walked down the church, gathering and looping the strong cord he had earlier laid along the floor, before securing the end of the now broken neck of Jesus. Loosening the heavy bolts had proven to be a lot simpler than he had imagined - given time the cross might have fallen down anyway.

He crept back through his living quarters and out to the front of the church. The coast was clear. He had not expected anybody to be about in any case at this ungodly hour.

Whistling softly to himself he opened the doors and decided it was time to call the police and inform them of the terrible tragedy. Jack did a little dance and clicked his heels in joy and anticipation of some good nights sleep and a long lie in from now on.

And indeed, he slept happily ever after.

A Story
for the Innocents

Time is of the essence

Nicholas jumped nervously at the sound of the hooter, signifying a change in shifts. Peering down from his perch in the glass covered office overlooking the vast production area, he was able to note that all of the lines were in operation.

Taking off his cap, he turned to face the calendar, whilst wiping the sweat from his brow. The perspiration trickled down through his wavy, grainy-lined face to drip slowly from his beard.

Crossing today's date from the calendar with a dark felt-tipped pen, Nicholas avoided looking at the production chart, knowing well that the continuous line was on a slow downward journey. There would never be enough time.

There was a loud bang, to be followed by a crashing sound emanating from the factory floor below him. Looking down, he observed that the driver of a forklift truck had hit and dented a wall of the factory which toppled the load over. As far as he could ascertain, nobody was hurt, but nevertheless he raced down the long stepped corridors, his weight and girth only allowing him a certain ungainly pace.

The red faced little man operating the forklift changed to a deeper shade of blush as Nicholas approached. Without waiting, he ran towards his boss, tears in his eyes, and apologised, dabbing at his eyes with a green handkerchief.

Nicholas was a kindly, giving man and his only immediate concern was the welfare of the workers, who, at this stage, were operating in shifts over seven days to help him achieve his enormous task. After reassuring the forklift driver and helping to reload the boxes, he ventured towards the far end of the factory to enter through a small door which contained the warm and comfortable stables. The animals ran towards Nicholas vying with each other in their attempts to nuzzle him and smother his face with slow stroking licks.

Nicholas looked at his stock and felt a tug of love at his heart which affected his breathing, causing him to swallow quickly in order to try to regain his composure. It would not do to have the boss seen in a light of weakness. The animals had never left him down, year after year performing heroically and ready to respond to his every direction, sometimes anticipating his manoeuvres, making it so much easier for him to do his work. After making sure that each in turn was fed and watered, he reluctantly returned to the hectic activity on the factory floor.

He jumped, his head hitting the slow slung lamp which hung over his desk. He had fallen asleep while again rereading the many demands, pleas, and requests from all over the world. His heart sank. There was no noise, no activity from the factory floor below him. Except for the dim lights over the emergency doors, the factory was in darkness.

They had left him in his hour of need. They had deserted him, but he could not blame them, because Nicholas had worked them very hard and to be fair they had given their all.

Taking the heavy bunch of keys from the top drawer of the ancient desk, he slowly made his way down the stairs to lock up, heavy in his heart.

In all his long years in the business, this had never happened before. Nicholas always prided himself on delivering punctually. There was nobody to blame except himself. The buck stopped here. Now it was all over. He raised his left hand to wipe away the tears of sadness running from his old eyes, while feeling for the light switch with his right. Maybe he was getting too old for this game. He must think about retirement.

The sudden burst of light which flooded the vast floor was accompanied by a long cheer and much clapping from the workers who were to be seen emerging in groups from their places of hiding. The crowd ran to him, attempting to jump up to kiss and cuddle him, some falling over only to get up again to form little circles and dance around the factory floor.

The head elf walked forward, his raised hand silencing the dancing, happy throng. Producing a voluminous tome containing the names of every boy and girl in the world, he placed it in the hands of Santa Claus and said *"Everything in order sir, your sleigh is ready, reindeers harnessed."*

Nicholas laughed loudly with relief. They all laughed while pushing and pulling at him in their attempts to help him to get to his sleigh.

Once aboard, he tied up the buttons of his long red coat and tightened the cord of his red fur-lined cap.

It was Christmas Eve and the children of the world were not to be disappointed.

The sleigh moved off, out through the large, open gate to rise slowly up into the glittering, star studded sky.

And Santa laughed and laughed and laughed.

Letters to Mike

Q. My Dear Michael,

I purchased your collection of so-called stories in a second-hand bookshop in Dublin (in fact they appear to have bought a joblot as the books were piled high on a dusty rickety table where the only buyer appeared to be myself). Nevertheless I went through the motions of reading your 'material.' I finished with a feeling of total disgust and sickness. The so-called 'stories' represent all that is wrong in our modern day society. I wouldn't even call them stories, to me they were the rantings of a snivelling cur. You deserve all the bad luck that is due to you. I am not including my name and address, but you can call me -

'No Fan,'
Cork.

A. Mother, I recognised your style straight away and would ask you to stop pestering me or I will be forced to call the police and have you arrested again. This is the last warning, I mean it!

M.

Q.   *Dear Mike,*

Please help me through this terrible period of my life. Two years ago I met and fell in love with a beautiful woman by the name of Clarissa. We hit it off immediately and spent all of our time together (except nights, because we decided to save ourselves for marriage). Things went swimmingly over the couple of years and we grew closer together and even more in love. We would often remove our contact lenses and gaze in the direction of each other's eyes while declaring our love, it was pure bliss. Then about three months ago we got married and it was on the night of the wedding that it all started. After the festivities ended we were at last alone in the bridal suite of the Hotel Pluto. We stood at each side of the bed and shyly began to undress. In my eagerness to get into bed I was first to be fully undressed. As soon as I turned around to face my beautiful bride with my arms extended waiting to embrace her, it started. She looked down at my pecker and laughed loudly, then she laughed some more. She held her stomach and tears ran down her cheeks as she tried to control her laughter but failed. (I can tell you this incident did not exactly boost my confidence). As the laughter got louder there were complaints from other hotel guests. The Duty Manager called for a Doctor to try and stop my beautiful wife's uncontrollable fits. He soon arrived, deciding to give her a sedative to stop the mirth. At that time I decided to go to the bathroom. As soon as I left the bedroom the laughter stopped and on re-entering it started up again. The Doctor noticed this and requesting that I leave the room again. I went to the bathroom and again the laughter halted, on re-emerging my wife burst into laughter again.

After tests it was discovered that my wife suffered from a condition called Humour and the sight of my small wrinkled thing only worsened that condition. We have now decided to call it a day and get divorced. This letter is written as a warning to all men with small things. On the first night, make sure to turn off the lights.

Signed,
Reduced Circumstances.

A.   This letter cheers me up no end. As the proud owner of a normal thing, I find it very difficult to empathise with you, but nevertheless I will try to help. I will send you the address of a plastic surgeon who is top notch at adding or subtracting, just mention my commission.

M.O'D.

Q.   *Dear Mike,*

My problem pertains to the perception of youth to people of my age group (I am aged one hundred and seven). Recently my youngest son, (he is aged seventy-four) stole the keys of my sports car in an attempt to stop me going to my job. I work as a stripper in a bar called 'The Last Chance Saloon,' and I feel that he is somehow ashamed of my occupation. I was able to thwart him by walking all of the two miles to the saloon, just getting there in time for the next night's performance. Also he is lately complaining a lot about my drug-taking, drinking and having rampant sex with anyone willing to pay. His constant sniping is really starting to annoy me and piss me off. Please help me.

Gloria Denude

Atlantic City

A.   *Dear Miss Denude*

I once had a dog called Chokey who was so intelligent that when handed a fine comb he could clean himself catching any intruder fleas on the side of the comb with the narrow teeth, he would then throw them on the floor and before they had a chance to hop, would pounce on them, with his front paws, killing them to death. Chokey lived to the ripe old age of seventeen, dying a clean death, but not before being awarded a brass medal from the W.H.O. for the elimination of one thousand, two hundred and thirty-seven fleas. I see you as Chokey, and your son as a flea. Get the message?

Yours in elimination,

M. O'D.

Q.   *Dear Mike,*

You might find it very strange to find out that this letter is being written by a monkey. My owner is a man of brilliance who taught me everything I know. I can sing, dance (having a preference for ballroom dancing) and drink and tell jokes with the boys in our local bar as good as the best of them. My dilemma is that my owner (a man by the name of Bob) is drinking rather a lot and insists on bringing me with him every time, and I now find that I now can outdrink him and finish up driving him home every night. My nerves are now very frayed and I suffer from a permanent hangover. I have the D.T.s and want to contact Alcoholics Anonymous but Bob stubbornly refuses to go and I can see us both finishing up in the gutter. What should I do?

(Name and address with Editor).

A.   *Dear Name and address with Editor,*

Anybody with any guts should have the balls to sign his name to a letter. Do you really expect a response writing anonymously (alcoholic or otherwise). Get with it sonny boy and come and live in the real world. If you want to live in the world of us humans, you drink like us humans and face the consequences. Anyway I never liked monkey business.

Mike O'Donovan (human being).

Q.   Dear Mike,

I work here in a circus as a trapeze artist by the stage name of 'The Human Eel and Mrs. Eel.' Of late I am getting a little big nervous. I think my wife has fallen for a clown, by the name of Dippity-Doo-Dah, who also has a trained seal and a wife. In his attempts to wave up at my wife while she flies around he has marked his face by hitting tent poles to such an extent that he now frightens the kids. My nervousness arises because I have a slight suspicion that my wife is out to murder me. Twice last week I found crushed glass in my elephant stew (Bessie the elephant died and the circus motto is waste not want not). Also I found my trapeze bar cut so as to break when I would grip it, but I was able to grab the ropes thereby saving my life. Also while I was rehearsing, the safety net was removed when I was not looking, luckily I fell on the fat lady and escaped death again.

Signed High Flyer,
No Fixed Abode.

A.   My razor sharp brain and my natural detective instincts combined to bring a sudden rush of blood to my head, so interested was I in this letter and my brilliant conclusion is based on pure logic. The simple fact is that your mind is working overtime and you seem quite paranoid. Everything as you explain it is purely coincidental. The glass obviously fell into the stew. Trapeze bars wear with age you know. As for the net, who knows? Was the fat lady singing at the time?

Yours in circusology,
Mike O'Donovan.

Q.   Dear Mike,

My problem is not really a problem, but I seek your opinion nevertheless. After marrying my childhood sweetheart we were blessed with two wonderful children, now grown up, he training to be a rocket scientist, and she an exceptionally talented writer and actress. My wonderful wife and I are immensely proud and content except for the fact that after thirty years as a vibrant heterosexual I have now found that I have a bent in the direction of homosexuality. This is extremely perplexing to me and I would like a solution to my predicament. I have always had a peculiar gait and without trying, I tended to sidle slightly to the left while directing my person in a straightforward direction. Could this have anything to do with my change of choice?

Signed 'Both Sides Now,'
Sydney.

A.   Does your daughter know of anybody in the film industry who might be interested in my stories? (or treatments as we in the business call them). Has she been in any movies I might know about? I am most anxious to find out if she has any useful contacts for me. You must also find that having a son as a rocket scientist is a great thing, what with possible free trips to the moon and all that. About your question - sorry no more space.

M. O'D.

Q.   We are a family of ducks living here in a pond just outside of town, and we have never threatened or harmed anybody in our lives. Our problem is that despite our placidity and our natural friendliness to everyone we are being shot at right left and centre, and we are getting sick and tired of the situation whereby anybody with a gun feels it is his or her duty to shoot at us. We are living in a world of dodge and weave, duck and dive and we are thoroughly sick of it. Our reason for writing this letter is to inform any shootists that we have decided on retaliation, with the help of some other feathery types. We have friends in high places. You have been warned.

Signed Bob Down, in the pond outside of Town.

A.   I am extremely annoyed with the tone of this letter, does the writer assume that just because he or it writes in a threatening way that it will stop legitimate hunters banging away at them to their hearts' content. Do you want to be a complete spoilsport and ruin others' fun. Was the letter actually written by a duck? More importantly, why the f**k am I replying to it as if it was written by something with webbed feet? On reflection, it could not have been written by a duck, where would they hold the pen?

Yours in sanity,
Mike O'Donovan.

Q.   *Dear Sir,*

The bars of the cell make it somewhat easier to write to you on this very sunny morning, as they shade the page beautifully, casting perfect straight lines for me to write across. It involves moving the page occasionally to follow the sun, but it is well worth it as you can observe as you read the perfect horizontal text. But I digress, my enquiry to you is about life outside of my place of confinement. I am due to be released in three weeks time having served my sentence of thirty years for the murder of a student of mine who was a very sloppy writer (I was a teacher at the time). I had admonished him on a number of occasions but he refused to heed me so I had no choice but to kill him, being a firm believer in corporal punishment. How are things out there? Will it be easy for me to assimilate back into society? Do you think that I will get my old job back? Could you put in a good word for me?

> *Yours in Anticipation,*
> *Bradbury Diplock, San Quentin.*

A.   *I find myself seething with anger and slightly frothing at the mouth on reading of this very obvious miscarriage of justice. The above cry for help from an educated man makes me want to sob, (but I am not that kind of person). What society needs are thousands of Bradbury Diplocks to enforce hard, strict obedience in every area of our 'society.' I will certainly assist you in any way I can. If I can not get you your old job back I will contact friends and get you something suitable to complement your talents. How does Iraq sound to you? Keep in contact and keep up the good work.*

> *Yours in Sympathy,*
> *Mike O'Donovan.*

201

"Thoughts From Down Under"

Q.   Dear Mike,

First of all I will preface my circumstances and situation before I ask your advice. My circumstances are that I am dead and have been in that condition for the past two years. My situation is just about ten feet under and here lies my problem, the cemetery where I lie is the most popular in town, a favourite drop-in point, if you like. There are so many funerals and visitors that I never get any rest in peace. You may imagine that the noise of tramping feet, crying, and last riting should not affect me, (being dead and all that), but it does, and at this stage I am shit sick of it. I have tried calling out, appealing for respect, but whenever I do call, the only responses I get are loud cries and the sound of running feet. Please help me out of my predicament as I feel that I am now at a dead end.

With eternal gratitude,
Denis Rolex.

A.   After reading your very interesting letter (twice) and scratching my head on a number of occasions (I suffer from a mild form of dandruff, which can be a bit of a devil at times, falling under the lapels of my tweed suit and also displaying itself on my green tie, sometimes covering it completely). I feel that I have a ready solution or two. First solution, you could apply to have your coffin moved down to say, ten feet, that could be of some help. Solution number two, I could apply to the authorities for an exhumation order to have your coffin (or what's left of it) shifted to a quieter graveyard. In the meantime just lie low, but do not take the intrusions lying down. Your query stands out as a beacon as to my popularity and fairmindedness. I welcome letters from the most brilliant, to the biggest dopes, from the living and the dead and others.

I remain, humane,
compassionate, (and alive),
Mike O'Donovan.

Q.   Dear Sir,

My work as a psychologist here in the State of Kentucky has given me a wonderful insight into the workings of the human mind. I am very successful in my profession, so much in fact that a lot of the opposition are now price-cutting in their attempts to take some of my patients. Despite all of this carry on, my customers have stuck with me. They might be mad, but not that mad because they, as I have often told them, realise that I am the very best. Even with the very healthy income deriving from my work I am very unhappy of late. I work long hours talking to an average of about sixteen nutters every day, five days a week and I find that, at times that I may be losing my sanity. I also find my mind wandering and wondering about things such as the composition and size of brake pads and how long it would take to roast an average size leg, and what kind of sauce should accompany it. Does any of this make any sense to you? Am I losing control? Is any of this normal?

Yours, And All That,
Sigmund Fraud.

A.   Dear Sigmund,

Please do not fret and worry yourself unnecessarily. It should reassure you to know that I myself have had similar thoughts for many years. I am in tip top mental shape, and never felt the need to see a shrink. Stop worrying and get on with the job of making money. You are as sane a man as I am.

Yours in moderation,
Mike O'Donovan.

Q.   Dear Mr. O'Donovan,

My problem is very complex yet very simple. I am a dancer travelling around the world with the famous driven dancers led by the charismatic and brilliant Michael Fately whose dancing, drinking, personality and loving are all the stuff of legend. So far we have travelled to every country in the world and filled vast arenas with multitude of fans all hoping to get a piece of Fately. We are the most popular line of dancers ever. Already there are plans to do shows from space platforms, and also a large stage is being built on the moon especially for some of the slower numbers. But I digress, my question to you is very simple - how can I get himself to fall in love with me? After all the years of travelling he has not once looked in my direction, or showed any signs of affection other than politeness and I am now at breaking point, should I approach him and declare my love or should I wait and bide my time. Please let me know soon as I am getting very fidgety. I have actually thought about suicide by jumping under Fately's feet during a show and making a dramatic and romantic exit from this world.

Yours in distraction, Chorus Liner.
P.S. I dream of Michael every night dancing and bouncing off the floor with those hard, hard shoes of his.
P.P.S. I speak with a lisp, do you think it could be something I said, in a certain way?

A.   Are you a man or a woman?
Mike O'Donovan.

Q.   Dear Mike,

I am the head of a Department based here in Brussels. My title is 'Commissioner for the Eradication of B.S.E.', a disease now rampantly spreading rapidly throughout the European Union, affecting cows in the main, as well as other parts. My problem is that we are receiving thousands of letters of complaint daily from where I can only describe as gutless, nervous, cranky, yellowbellied, fainthearted, cowardly, miserable bastards (and that's only the children). The complaints I refer to accuse me of not acting fast enough in banning animal feed containing other animals. As a regular meat eater myself I never could see wrong with this practice. It was only after some pressure from my grandmother, a lady I adore and cherish that I decided to act. Now, I find that I am being berated by some of my friends in the animal feed business and also by some of the greedy farmers. I now feel squeezed in like a beef burger between two opposing buns. What should I do?

Yours in anticipation,
André Tercel.
Brussels.

A.   I find myself seething with anger on reading the above. My first response is what are the parents doing while their children are engaged in writing such spiteful and vicious letters, is there no control anymore? My second response is a little bit similar only longer - bigger idiot you to listen to your grandmother and be influenced by an old crock. What if beef is banned altogether? What will I do to satisfy my long love affair with corned beef? Think about that you cribbers! On reflection I believe that beef will never be banned, the bucks are too big. What does B.S.E. mean?

Yours droolingly,
Mike O'Donovan

Q. *Dear Mike*

I have recently been elected President of the greatest country in the world called America, and I am in a bit of a quandary as to who I should bomb first. I write this letter knowing and appreciating your tremendous lack of candour and honesty and would appreciate your input and direction.

George Doudlya Bush,
The White House,
Washington (DC)

A. *Dear George,*

I do not usually respond to people with crossed eyes but because of your elevated boots and positionI will make an exception this time. George, always go for the darker colours and make sure then live in countries far from home. Your bombs and gun would, I assume, have long range capabilities. If the off colours live far enough away you can kill to your hearts content as they would not have a chance in hell at attempting retaliation. Also be wary of nations who do not conform to western dress codes and desrve the odd air strike. Best of luck to you and the big oil companies in your endeavour in changing the face (and seasons) of this wonderful world of ours
                    Your in total admiration
                    Mike O'Donovan

Q.   Dear Mike,

I am penning this letter in a last desperate attempt to once and for all quell the rumours and talk about me and my situation vis-a-vis life and death. I would like to inform the general public once and for all that I am well and truly dead and intend to stay that way. Supposed sightings of me in places such as Medugorjie, Hanks Hamburger Joint, in the queue at Graceland, busking outside the White House or working in Herlihy's Hot Dog Manufacturing Plant are, to say the least, false and damaging to my reputation. You, Mike are the only person I would trust to write to on this subject, knowing of your reputation, for fair-mindedness and honesty. Hoping that you will pass on this message of fact to your many billions of readers.

> *Yours sincerely,*
> *Elvis Aaron Presley*
> *(All Puffed Up)*

A.   Dear Elvis,

It is indeed a pleasure to hear from you. I, of course, as a man of tremendous knowledge and all things like that always fully appreciated the fact that you are dead. I will indeed pass on this information to my legions of followers out there in the big wide world and beyond. On a personal note I would have thought that when you were alive you should have given up singing and stuck to acting as I always admired the way you refused to bow to circumstances and the very obvious poor direction in all your brilliantly acted movies. Whether they were comedy scenes or tragidrama you always kept the same facial wooden look on that handsome intelligent countenance of yours. If you were not dead I would have asked you around for tea. I would now like to inform my multitudes of readers that Elvis has well and truly left the building.

> *I remain,*
> *Mike O'Donovan,*
> *Advisor to the Celebrities.*

207

Q.   Sir,

With reference to a recent letter from Elvis Presley, a dead singer, I wish to protest strongly. I myself am a singer of notes having had years and years and years of success and until now, despite the fact that I am still barely alive, have never resorted to writing to a hack such as yourself for advice on any fxxxxxg thing until fxxxxxg now. Being a committed Christian I do not usually resort to using such vulgar fxxxxxg language but the letter from Elvis really pxxxxd me off. Just because Elvis the pxxxk has not had a top ten hit now for quite a while makes us fxxxxxg think that his fxxxxxg reason for writing to you is all part of a fxxxxxg career move on the part of his fxxxxxg record company and you for your part should stop publishing letters from dead fxxxxxg people in any fxxxxxg case.

> *Sir Cliff Richard,*
> *Old, weary and pxxxxd off.*

A.   Deary, deary me, Cliffie seems to be a bit upset, so upset that he refers to me as a hack. I am in fact a highly respected writer with an impeccable reputation world wide and refuse to take such vulgar crap from anybody. Your vicious response to a letter from a dead great actor and singer only shows envy and lack of self-confidence. If I had the choice to listen to you or a croaking frog I would pick the frog. Put that in your pipe and smoke it.

> *Yours in decent language,*
> *Mike O'Donovan.*

Q. Dear Mike,

My problem is onefold, first is my tricky relationship with a certain American President called George, who got me to play a game called 'Bomb Iraq.' I agreed to play this game only because I think that if I don't my friend George might bomb me instead. My second problem is my unnatural admiration and love for Margaret Thatcher, even though I realise that she is as mad as a hatter and always was. I have no qualms about bombing Iraq or any other oil spoiling country for that matter, the problem there is that my friend George is now suggesting that since we are so close we should start dating. I also have a recurring dream about Margaret Thatcher dressed in the uniform of a Nazi Stormtrooper hitting me on the head with a dead monkey and I find this slightly disturbing. So Mike, what should I do about George? Should I stop accepting his calls or should we come out and publicly declare our special relationship?

Yours in a quandary,
Tony Blare.

A. Dear Tony,
Methinks you fret too much. Firstly, both George and his daddy are known to suffer from chronic constipation and that condition has been known to cause involuntary pressing of buttons while motivating the sufferer to shout 'Bombs Away,' thus working as a cheap laxative, so try and be understanding of their faults. As regards your special relationship, I do not want to know the murky details but as in any courtship it takes two to tango, so watch your step. With reference to your reference regarding Margaret Thatcher, I would not worry too much about your dreams about her as I have dreams myself something akin to yours, except that in my case she is dressed as Ivan The Terrible holding a sword while on horseback and charging towards me. Luckily I always wake up in time. So you see Tony, you are as normal as I am.
Best wishes for your future droppings,

Happy to be of service,
Mike O'Donovan.

Q.   *Dear Mike,*

I write this request to you knowing of your interest in animal welfare and your humanitarian ways and believe that you should be awarded the Nobel Prize for animal welfare. My problem is that I am the proud owner of both a Pitbull terrier and a Pekinese, each of them being a credit to the doggy world, but the Pekinese is the most vicious little bastard of a dog I have ever encountered. I know in my heart that he is a gentle soul but he tends to project the wrong image by biting me at any opportunity he gets. I have paid for sessions for him to attend an animal physiologist but to no avail. I would like to keep him, but at the present time he is proving to be a right pain in the butt, what should I do?

Signed Two Leads Kelly,
Albuquerque.

A.   *This is a most interesting query. I used to own a beautiful Golden Spaniel once myself until I came home one night after a few drinks on the town, and to impress my (then) girlfriend I threw him out of the window, (I live on the twenty-fifth floor). Unfortunately he did not survive the impact as he struck the spiked railings surrounding the building. He died. My advice to you is lock both of your pets in a room for one week without food and your problem should be resolved. Think about it. Let me know which dog survives.*

"Let us paws" Ha Ha.
Mike O'Donovan.

Q. Dear Mike,

Please help me in my simple endeavour. My wish is to appear on the pages of 'Shallow' magazine, a publication I am quite sure that an international figure like yourself would be very much aware of. I eagerly await its delivery to my local newsagents and once I get my trembling hands on its sweet-smelling shiny pages I am immediately transported to wonderland. I envy the beautiful acne free faces and places that the rich and infamous possess. Beautiful drawing rooms, perfect teeth and children, manicured nails and lawns. Beautiful women displaying eye boggling cleavage. Handsome men wearing expensive tasteful clobber, and vice versa. Wealth, prosperity and happiness, they are my simple goals, the problem is that I am poverty stricken. I buy my clothes in second hand shops and my face has often been described as very plain verging on ugly. Also I live in a kip. What are my changes in appearing in the wonderful 'Shallow' mag?

> *Yours in anticipation,*
> *Clarence Chance,*
> *The bedsit above Wong's Takeaway,*
> *Dog and Cat Walk,*
> *Liverpool.*

A. When will you get it into your thick heads that I only welcome letters from achievers and rich people? I am sick and tired of the whinging and crying of losers like you. Get a life Clarence or better again, don't. I would kindly ask the poor not to take up valuable space on my page. Now F.O.

Mike O'Donovan.

Q. Dear Mike,

I hope you have a solution to my little query. I have always had a deep and abiding love of animals. In fact I qualified as a veterinarian in my quest to help our dumb friends and all that. I lately achieved my dream of working and helping my friends by getting a job in a zoo. Some of my happiest moments are spent in the animal houses, shovelling dung while singing 'Animal Crackers In My Soup.' There are seventeen different species of exotic birds on exhibition, forty six types of animals and aquatic things, and seven different sorts of reptiles. The problem is one of the three alligators, a female by the name of Alice is extra friendly to me. I was recently attacked by all three alligators and suffered the loss of my right arm. While they were attacking me I noticed that Alice held back while the other two frenziedly tore at my arm. Alice came to attack me only at the last minute and appeared to be happy enough just to bite off my fingers. After coming out of hospital I went back to work at the zoo, a better and lighter man. Whenever I go to attend at the reptile enclosure, Alice stares at me and winks a lot. Do you think she fancies me, and what are my chances?

Signed, Leftie MacDonald.

A. Get off my page you pervert.
M.O'D.

Q. Dear Mike,

It is with no regret that I have to inform you that I have decided include your Green Isle on my hit list of evil axis countries, despite simpering support or your Teashack Bartery Ahern. The lack of support for me in the two elections by Irish Americans have forced my christian hand and we have decided to kill you all. We will then go after any politicians who are left alive and impose democracy and freedom by giving them leadership titles and set up a police force which will be totally controlled by us. I have evangelically decided on the old eye for an eye policy and will use my christian forces to bomb the shit out of your country. By the way my best wishes to your president Michael Flatley. I must finish now as my speech therapist Arnold Schwarzenegger has arrived.

Yours in God and Oil
George W. Bush

Dear George,

If I was living in the United States I personally would have voted for you as often as possible. So, as a longtime admirer of yours and your great brain I would ask you not to bomb my house (it is marked in red in the enclosed map). Feck my neighbours, none of them like you anyway so they deserve what they get

P.s I don't care what they say, I do not think you are that great a dope.

M O'Donavan

Q.   *Dearie,*

My question pertains to people who avail of the sex industry and the very sick minds they have. I work as a sex telephonist offering advice and dirty talk or whatever chit-chat is required. The problem is all of my callers don't even talk about sex, they ask me questions on where to go on holidays, they talk about the weather, my impressions of George Bush, B.S.E., the schools education system, fashion, different brands of washing up liquid and which is the best. Also the American Star Wars project, tomato growing, accountancy, soliciting in the courts, conservation, interior decor and other such mundane topics. I am getting really peeved off by all of the stupid questions, also the situation as it exists could hurt my chances of promotion to a more elevated position within the company. What do you think, dearie, what should I do?

Confidentially Yours,
Gloria Hunnysuckle.

A.   *Dear Cheapie,*

Judging by the tone of your letter you lack balls, but of course if you are a woman that is quite understandable, if you are a man you're in serious trouble. Anyway, I will get on with my remarkable response, as indeed are all of my responses. As a person of brilliant perception I recognise the problem straight away and my fast brain sends a message to me for you. The message is - you are a tart, pure and simple. Do not ever refer to me as dearie again or I will make sure that you will never be able to lift a phone again (or anything else for that matter).

Mike O'Donovan.

Q.   Dear Señor Mike,

My problem is very complex one. My local cantina contains three pool tables which are always in use, consequently there is usually confusion regarding the position of the balls. I will explain further, the three tables in question are set very close together so as to make room for dancing, so close in fact that the balls tend to hop from table to table causing total confusion to the players. Also there is discrimination to those people of the fat variety who cannot squeeze between the tables. This has caused much resentment among the fat ones who have turned against us of the skinny persuasion and have threatened violence. Is there any solution to this problem? At a public meeting attended by all of the local people it was decided to write to you as a last resort.

Signed Steve Lavender,
Wall Street, N.Y.

A.   I actually rang my grandmother (who is half Peruvian and half alive). She was World Pool Champion in Eighteen Ninety Nine and World Skateboarding Champion the following year and is a very wise woman. On explaining your predicament to her she thought for a moment, before keeling over and dying. You have the death of a very fit lady of only one hundred and twenty four on your hands. When I catch up with you, you are a dead man. Otherwise, best wishes.

Mike O'Donovan.

Q.   Dear Mike,

My story is a tale of woe but I will try to be as bright as I can under the circumstances. My wife Alberta lately left me and our two lovely drug-ridden skin headed children. She had complained on and off, about the size of my pecker for a good number of years now, but I took it all in my stride, because as you well know every marriage has its little ups and downs and there is always a certain amount of friction. What really annoys me is the fact that my wife left me for another woman who has no pecker at all, what would you make of all of this? Anyway my mother always told me that size does not matter, its which brand of cigarettes you smoke afterwards.

Yours in anticipation,
Please Advise Me,
Raoul Pinchbeck.

A.   Raoul,

Life can be a very funny thing, please stay with me while I philosophise and practise some yoga and stuff. Aah, that feels better. Now what was your problem again? It's okay, I have it now. It had been suggested that there were in fact two inventions relating to water powered engines over the past twenty years and that all the oil companies bought the patients and the inventors together, thus destroying any hopes of a cleaner environment. But speaking personally as an investor in Traxo Oil I couldn't give a tupenny f**k. Cheers.

Mike O'Donovan

Q.   Dear Mike,

I must express my tremendous satisfaction after reading your brilliant, remarkable, sympathetic analysis and understanding of the human condition. Your knowledge and grasp of complicated defects and failings such as bunions, sweaty hands, politics, lack of height, nervous tics, sheep fancying, urine consumption, dancing, not being white, quiche eating, Concorde flying, soap watching, catharsis, atheism, liking people, dog loving, knife and fork using, having large bushy eyebrows, monacle wearing, head shaving, reading etc. etc. I could go on and on, singing your praise but I will trespass just a little more on your page to congratulate you on one particular brilliant and intelligent response, explaining why ladders contain rungs. Your answer was precise and definite, explaining the process with compassion, step by step. Is there anything that you don't know?

Yours admiringly,
Wesley Crood,
Croods Takeaway,
Caucasiatown,
Shanghai.

A.   I don't know!

Yours in usual puzzlement,
Mike O'Donovan

Q. I have perceived a noticeable lack of direct response to questions sent to you on anything of a gay nature. Your lack of candour in answering on the nature of the above leaves me to think that you have something to hide. Just what is your problem regarding same, is it something in your past? Please do not ignore this honest request and give me a straight answer to a straight question and do not be evasive, as you have been in past responses.

Yours expectantly,
Don Quang,
Chinatown,
Beijing.

A. In my many walks through the forest of life I have observed and witnessed many climatic changes and seasons. The dropping of squirrels nuts and autumn leaves can be immensely interesting or not, depending on one's interest in either. The same applies to the setting sun particularly if there is a backdrop of a clear red sky, blood red is a most attractive colour. To some people who cannot tell east from west and are confused as to which is dawn and which is dusk it can be a terrible cross to bear as to not know whether to go to bed or get out of it. Also, I believe that speed limits should be eliminated completely, what with a growing world population and so many extra mouths to feed it would make it a little bit easier if there were more serious crashes.

Hoping you are happy with this response of clarity,
Mike O'Donovan.

Q.   Dear Mike,

I am completely friendless and companionless and nobody likes me, but in fairness they have very good reason not to. You see, I am a man of extremely cranky disposition and I just happen to like it that way. Being sour and grumpy means that nobody asks me for anything, anyway even if I was not grumpy nobody would get anything from me in any case. Both my dear departed mother and father were blessed with horribly depressing personalities and I had a rotten but happy childhood. As I write this letter I am wondering why I am making the effort at all as I despise you as much as I despise anybody else. Anyway, I digress, my reason for contacting you is simple. I am interested in joining or forming a club where others of my ilk could meet for social occasions and not talk. Much as I hate having to ask anything of anybody I bow before your superior stupidity and detestingly request that use your network of idiotic connections to assist me.

Yours scathingly,
Rupert Wilk,
Professor of Communications,
University of Lugubriousness.

A.   Dear Mister Wilk,

I can fully appreciate people's dislike of you. After reading your letter I myself find that I have no time for you whatsoever. Regarding your request about a club I can only suggest that you procure one and beat yourself to death, slowly. Do not ever call me names again, or you will die to regret it.

Okay Lumphead!
Mike O'Donovan.

Q.   *Dear Mike,*

We pen this letter in an attempt to gain some information as to go about invading a country. The country in question being Norway. Why Norway you might ask? My answer is, why not! The beauty of the whole scene is that nobody knows anything whatsoever about the place including myself and my comrades. There are now three of us and growing fast. We have perused the tabloids for many months now and yet have to see a mention of the word 'Norway' in any shape or form, so if an invasion were to take place who the hell would know about it! We seek your assistance in procuring things like maps, arms, boots and woolly hats for our heads. They, of course, would have to have holes on the front, otherwise we would not be able to see or breathe. We have burned the midnight oil on many an occasion plotting and planning (particularly when the electricity was cut off) and our request to you is simple, can you assist us in our endeavours?

We sign our names and titles with pride,
Richard Bole, Conductor (No. 87 Bus),
Adrian Kepple, Master Balloon Blower,
Freddy Fluck, Head Cycle Attendant.

A.   *My dear Richard, Adrian and Freddy,*

I think your idea is absolutely fantastic. If I was younger and more stupid I would certainly have liked to join you in your venture but alas I can not. Also my money is tied up with pensions and things like that. If you ever get to the invadee country please tell me where it is.

Yours in admiration,
Mike O'Donovan.

Q.   Dear Mike

I am a very successful businessman and am much noted and admired by myself and my family. My interests lie in publishing, beans, making as many zillions as I possibly can and collecting titles. My first title was plain 'Mister' but I was never entirely happy with that so I pulled some strings, dished out some beans to the right people and eventually I was awarded an Honorary Doctorate. You may think that I would be happy to be called 'Doctor' by all of my subordinates, but no, my newish wife and I decided that if I also took up British Citizenship I could score even better. Then, lo and behold, without any prompting from me whatsoever I was made a 'Sir' by the Queen of England. My problem is that now people are calling me names and bestowing unwanted titles on me like 'pompous ass,' 'dickhead,' 'ego-inflated prick' and 'narcissist.' How should I respond to those of low class with obvious peasant background?

Yours humbly (ha ha),
Sir Anthony O'Really.
P.S.: As I write this short note of humility a case of beans is winging its way to your good self, Sir A. O'R.

A.   Dear Sir Anthony,

I am at this point in time responding to your query while sitting on my toilet seat. In the future please try to make sure that the letter arrives ahead of the beans. Consuming such quantities of beans is proving to have quite an effect on the ozone layer and I am developing quite a musical rear end to boot. I now find that I am out of toilet paper and will have to use your letter to good effect. I salute you and thank you for this note of usefulness.

Yours hurriedly,
Mike O'Donovan.

Q.   Dear Mike,

If I could take some space in your publication to beseech you to help me out of a serious dilemma. I work as an embalmer for a top undertaker and take much pride in my work. When I work I give everybody my all, without exception. My handiwork embodies and personifies everything a good embalmer should be. The product is wheeled into me in a very pale and sometimes rotten condition, but always finishes up looking happy and contented with a fragrant knockout smell and rosy cheeks. Two years ago my employer hired a young apprentice by the name of Walter Fudd and ordered me to teach him the art of stuffing and primping dead people. Walter took to the business like a duck to water and in his enthusiasm and youth, succeeded so well that he can now outdo me, stuffing two bodies for every one of mine. Last week he was promoted and now has the official title of Head Stuffer and has his choice of the body pick (always choosing the smaller and easier ones). Do you not think that it is ironic that I taught him everything he knows and now he has his choice of coffins and orders me about, treating me like a serf?

Please help,
Wilbur Ripple.

A.   My dear Wilbur, it is indeed ironic that callous youth should overtake experience but if you take the letter 'y' away from irony what are you left with? Get something weighty and blunt and dispatch Walter Fudd to join those on wheels. This may seem like an old-fashioned remedy but believe you me it has proven to be a tried and tested solution over the years.

Yours in fraternity,
Mike O'Donovan.

Q.   Dear Mike,

I recently read an article in the Readers Digress on the phenomena of UFO's and it stated that aliens are already among us. There were also some horrible and grotesque photos of beings which it claimed were not of this world. If the said article is true does it mean the end of humanity as we know it? The written text was very frightening but the photographs were absolutely stomach churning and disgusting. I am enclosing a copy of the piece and images for your perusal and comment.

Yours in fright,
Dick Dundun,
Dundee.

A.   After reading your letter and the supplied article I have come to the conclusion that the photos are indeed very scary but the beings as shown have been with us for a long time manifesting themselves in the shape of lawyers, politicians and bankers who survive off the backs and blood of humans. This does not mean, of course, that they should not be let live but I think that they should all be locked up in a large enclosure for humans to view, throw them some peanuts and watch them at their predatory games. Alternatively they could all be rounded up, tortured and then sent back to the planet smug. I hope this response gives you some food for thought.

Yours in anticipation,
Mike O'Donovan.

Q.   Comrade Mike,

Please help me in a very difficult situation. My name is Marcos and I am the leader of a movement called the Zapatistas. While I am very happy to be leader of a downtrodden and dispossessed people like the Mayan's I now find that I am becoming something of a folk hero and this is something which I am totally against, being a man of modesty and humility. My main adversary is a wily politician by the name of Fox who has perfected the art of double-dealing. His government has been involved in a number of talks with us and all he had to offer were free small bottles of Coca-Cola to the many thousands of political prisoners held in his jails. What do you think? Do you think that we should accept his offer or hold out and demand the large family size bottles of that most delicious and nourishing tipple. I also write some thought provoking poetry, here is a sample

There once was a dickhead called Fox
Who was destined to end in a box
He tried sailing a boat
But the boat wouldn't float
'cause like Fox it was short of a cox.

Subcommandante Marcos,
Somewhere in Mexico.

A.   *I do not usually respond to communications from Rebel Leaders but having read of the many great achievements of the wonderful charismatic President Vincente Fox I am forced to make an exception in this case. Try and get it into you thick head, globalisation is in, indigenuity is out. Are you aware that during President Fox's time with Coke, sales rose by almost one third, and culling increased by fifty percent, thus further increasing profits for that wonderful multinational company of Happy Santa's and well fed investors. As one who would trust Vincente with my last bottle of sweet bubbly water I would advise you to do the same. Anyway, did you ever ask*

224

yourself as to why the socially deprived are socially deprived? I'll tell you why! Because they deserve to be, that's why! My response is based on logic, common sense and brains.

Yours in fury,
Mike O'Donovan.

P.S. I liked your poetry. MOD

Q. Dear Mike,

I write this letter as a matter of supreme urgency and while not wishing to jump the queue I would appreciate if you could fastrack this most pressing dilemma. I am the driver of a highspeed locomotive, in other words, I drive a train. Of late our superiors have been encouraging us to take up a hobby as a means of easing the stress caused by our most mind consuming profession. Some drivers have taken up badminton, others went for knitting and embroidery, transpotting, modelling, jigsaw puzzling, body building, painting, glue sniffing, standing, serial killing and other such pastimes. In my particular case I decided to start to imbibe in alcohol. Up to that time I was always teetotal but as I said to myself 'what the heck, try anything once.' Thereby hangs a tale. I found that drink, any kind of drink, suits me admirably, so much in fact that I am now half pissed to fully pissed all of the time and am finding it difficult to focus my mind on anything other than my new-found hobby. Occasionally, just for the fun of it, I will brake sharply causing the train to jolt to a sudden halt. On hearing the screams and wails of lily livered passengers I find myself laughing and gloating at the discomfort and injuries I cause. Am I being somewhat irrational in my activities or would you think that I am run of the mill. Am I going off the rails?

Yours in speed,
Oscar Siding.

A. My dear Oscar,

Your wild self-moralising will soon drive you round the bend if you don't keep things on track. Of all the other activities you mention, yours appear to be the healthiest and most interesting of the lot. Speaking as an occasional train user I find that journeying by that particular means of *transport can be pretty humdrum, particularly since they eliminated that marvellous trance inducing 'clickety clack.' I am quite sure that despite the injuries some passengers might suffer you are a lot better off bringing some excitement to their boring lacklustre safe existences. All that drinking is changing you into a man of daring and innovation. Anyway, caring is for wimps. Keep up the good work.*

Bottoms Up,
Yours in soulmating,
M. O'Donovan.

Q.   Dear Mike,

My burning ambition is to be a poet. When I was young my teacher told me that I had a gift for poetry and I always write at least one poem each day in tribute to that marvellous teacher of perception. Reading your material has convinced me that you possess the heart of a poet yourself and so I include a pair of poems for your comments. Here goes -

(1)

There was a young lady from Paris
Who had a habit of falling on her aris
Cooks crow at night
So let's have a fight
De Dom, De De Dom, De De Daris.

(2)

The grass which grows in a field
Is something accompanied by weeds
But I can only assume its better
When good seeds are sent by post in a letter.

They are just two of my better poems out of many thousands I have written. What do you think, Mike?

Dylan John Thomas,
Swansea.

A.   Dear Mister Thomas,

I weep in ecstasy at your tender extrapolation of humanity as expressed in your touching sonnets, but my heart also glows with warm pride in so far that you have picked me to expose your talents to the world. My answer is to give up your day job whatever it may be. Any sane publisher would give his (or her) right arm and more, to put your wonderful lyrics in *what is sure would be a best selling book.*

I salute you and thank you.
Mike O'Donovan.

Q.   Your heart-warming response to my last communication gave me great encouragement, so much in fact that I have decided to send some more of my poems for your delight and enjoyment.

Poem 1
I don't believe in reading dictionaries
They can easily fall and damage your knees
They are easy for people of heavy girth
I personally prefer comics to be read by the hearth.

Poem 2
Flowers mostly bloom in the spring
Is that fair to the other seasons?
I prefer apples and grapes myself
For obvious dietary reasons.

Poem 3
It is said that cars run on petrol and diesel
And flying saucers on what we don't know at all
But despite all is said or whoever is read
I never saw a car running.

Poem 4
I like going to visit a second-hand shop
Where a purchase can dress you up like a fop
For whatever the colour while your hands on the rudder
Your trousers, while held up, will never drop.

I could go on and on Mike, but the reason I included the four new poems for you to read is because I welcome your interpretation of my works, knowing of your vast knowledge of the arts.

Dylan John Thomas,
Swansea.

230

A.   I gasp with admiration on reading your magnificent poems. All I can say is that if you were a painter your ear would be well cut off by now. For once I am speechless.

Mike O'Donovan.

Q.   *Dear Mr. O'Donovan,*

The omnipresence of patrician patriots has ensured that the jingoism of the pleiades in taurus, repair our faith in mankind in a very recoupetory way. The very essence of the understanding of the tree of sassafras is as sound as a sarcophaqus in the cold of night. To savour the acrid salty taste which is the Sargasso is one of the ultimate delights surely. One could also similituded as something else. To change your appearance with the help of a little Kohn might be seen as more than a little vain. Do not attempt to climb the Lignum Vitae without a reason. The massif stand together, united in solidarity looking down on us in a majestic way. The opulence some of the opus's is quite abundant as shown in the oracles of old. Despotism, enslavement, subjugation, all can be overt in a peculiar way but each should dance to it's own tune, provided each can dance. The poltroons of the property propositioners indent on our sensibilities to the propitiousners of all. I will finish this short statement of question by asking - Did you understand any of the above, Mr. Knowall O'Donovan?

Yours In Comprehension,
Alfredo De Marke,
University of Cognition.

A.   *I warned you smartasses before, stop using big words. I am a plain spoken man without a need to try to impress people. You should try it sometime, prick.*

Michael O'Donovan.

232

Health and Beauty

Q.   *Dear Mike,*

I have only been waiting for someone of your calibre to start such a column, thank you. My problem involves a particular part of my face, my forehead to be exact. In the very centre of the same said forehead lies my problem. The problem is in the shape of a wart, a very large wart which appears to be growing by the day. I was advised by my doctor to apply a liquid which he claimed would burn the bugger off, but it only added fuel to the fire, because it grew some more and is now more prominent than ever. Only this morning I measured it to discover that it now stands four inches from its base. It is very handy as a shade on a sunny day but it's not so clever in the rain, holding water to drop on my face long after the skies have cleared. The position is as I have stated, wart and all. Hoping that you can offer a solution to my intrusive protuberance.

Sylvia Stubs,
Calgary.

A.   *My Dear Sylvia,*

You will be glad to hear that I have decided not to drink while responding to healthy and beauty freaks such as yourself. I laughed a lot when I first read your letter but I soon had to stop because I was getting cramps in my stomach. Your very obvious paranoia is very amusing. Sylvia, you must learn to be positive and also learn to use your laughable defect in some useful way. Think woman, think. You could always conduct a band simply by nodding your head in time to the music. It could be used as a very useful weapon in stabbing someone. Have you considered fencing? You could easily play the part of a unicorn in some show or other. If you played the fiddle, you would not even need a bow. So you see Sylvia your complaint only puts you in the shade, ha ha. If it grows anymore please let me know as I may have more solutions, who knows.

Yours from a distance,
Mike O'Donovan
P.S.: One a more serious note have you considered using a blowtorch? ...
MOD

Q.   Dear Mike,

My problem pertains to the problem of constipation in flight. You see, I work as an Air Hostess and believe you me it is a very demanding job what with rushing around serving plastic food in plastic containers and serving drinks and things. I fear for my job of late as I now spend most of my time sitting in the toilet seat of the plane, without results. My co-workers are now complaining about having to do my work for me. I also feel giddy and bloated because of my inability to offload my cargo. What should I do Mike, please help me.

Yours sincerely,
Claudette Bowles.

A.   Buy two pounds of streaky bacon, put it into a pot of water and bring it to the boil, by allowing one hours boiling for every pound it should take about two hours in total. Remove it from the pot immediately. You then stuff the hot pot with as much cabbage as you possibly can, adding breadsoda to soften the shit out of it. In the meantime try to avoid slicing thin attractive strips off the delicious streaky and shoving it into your gob. I know it will be very tempting but it defeats the whole purpose of my response to you.

NEXT STAGE - Dice the bacon into small squares. Do not worry if the bacon is hairy, stage three takes care of that and other growths.

STAGE THREE - Obtain a large mixer or blender and throw the bacon pieces and cabbage in together and mix them to feck until you finish up with what will look like green cement. You must allow the mix to rest for at least two days, then you reheat and keep it on simmer for another day. You then test it out on the cat, if he purrs and is still alive you are in luck, the concoction is perfect. Allow to cool, then fill a large mug with the mixture, you will need *a knife and fork and of course a serviette. One mug a day for a week should clear out both yourself and your pot.*

SIDE AFFECTS - If there are any complaints regarding foul smells on board your plane just try to keep on the move and spread both the smell and the blame around.

I am glad and relieved to be of assistance to another being of the human variety and I promise to always help my fellow man provided the envelopes they send me contain enough cash to provide for a decent meal for two plus a bottle of wine and a tip.

Mike O'Donovan.

(Afterthought - If all fruit fails you could try a bent coathanger or if it's a really hard job I would suggest a hammer and chisel ...